BERGERAC

By the same author

The Bernard Shaw Companion (with Mollie Hardwick)
The Chinese Detective
The Four Musketeers
The Inheritors
The Man Who Would Be King
Mrs. Hudson's Diaries
On with the Dance
The Private Life of Sherlock Holmes
Regency Royal
Upstairs, Downstairs

BERGERAC

Michael Hardwick

based on the BBC-TV Series
created and produced by
Robert Banks Stewart

St. Martin's Press
New York

LCC: 82-60186
ISBN: 0-312-07576-6

First published in Great Britain by the British Broadcasting Corporation

First U.S. Edition
10 9 8 7 6 5 4 3 2 1

C. 1

M

The publishers would like to thank Robert Banks Stewart, John Kershaw, Alistair Bell and Bob Baker for the use of their scripts in preparing this book.

Chapter One

As midnight approached, the sounds of revelry from establishments along the St Helier waterfront diminished. Laughter and the slamming of car doors were less in evidence. Only the overloaded bass in one persistent disco thud-thudded above the gentle slap of calm sea against the hulls of yachts, cabin cruisers, catamarans, dinghies, and the buoys and ropes securing them.

A few late strollers still moved: young couples, holding each other closely, pausing to kiss and gaze out at the darkling scene of bobbing masts and stays against starlight, then kissing again and meandering on.

The townsfolk were abed, as at this time on most nights. In hotels and boarding-houses, several thousand tourists did not begrudge the loss of a few hours from their packages of sun and safe swimming, good eating, cheap booze, and un-pestered sightseeing in surroundings comfortingly British yet redolent of France. They slept secure, protected in this English-speaking foreign-feeling Channel Island by a lieutenant-governor appointed by Her Majesty and an efficient police force, independent of any outside jurisdiction but fully linked to the sophisticated resources of Scotland Yard.

Unnoticed by the romantic wanderers at the harbour's edge, one of the members of the Jersey States Police CID slouched in plain clothes in the driving seat of a car, stationed unobtrusively in deep shadow. His eyelids were heavy, so that he had to keep blinking them hard to hold his con-centration as he went on watching one particular boat, moored to the harbour wall.

It was a fishing trawler of chunky build, tough enough to spend days at sea in any weather, with capacious fuel tanks for a long voyage. It had berths for four and a galley well stocked with food and drink. Detective Sergeant Jim Bergerac knew this, because he had been aboard, and seen for himself.

A drugs squad officer had gone with him. While Bergerac had poked around generally, and kept an eye open for the approach of any of the crew, the other had searched minutely. He had found nothing. Ensuring that no sign of their visit would be noticed, he had left. Bergerac had stayed, in the car in the shadows.

It was logical to deduce that since the cargo was not yet aboard, the crew would be bringing it with them. It might occupy no more than one innocuous hold-all; but in whatever country it was intended for it would be worth a million to someone and would push an incalculable number of others a step closer to degradation and even death.

So Jim Bergerac blinked his eyes and watched. At the first sight of any of that crew he would radio in. Enough reinforcements for a board-and-search party would be sharing the shadows with him inside minutes, waiting till all four crew had got aboard and the risk of a premature swoop would have passed.

He had sat cramped there for three hours. Because at least one of the men would know him by sight, he had to stay in the car, rather than go and lean on the railing. If he had been able to do that, he might have seen all four of them creep aboard, not from the harbourside, but from a dinghy whose approach had been invisible from his present viewpoint.

The first he knew that everything was going wrong was the roar of the starting engine and a puff of smoke from the vertical exhaust pipe abaft the cabin. There was a momentary glimpse of a face as a man reached up to slip the mooring rope.

Jim groped for the R/T microphone. He wasted precious seconds because it had slipped between the empty passenger seat and his own. He pressed the button. Without regard for procedure, or waiting for acknowledgment that he was being heard, he yelled his message.

6

He let the instrument fall from his hand and wrenched at the door handle, at the same time pushing hard with his shoulder. It was a clumsy movement. As the door jerked open he went with it, almost falling out. He saved himself, cursing, and got onto his feet. But he reeled as he started to run, and his dash to the harbour edge was anything but fleet-footed.

The boat was under way, its engine roaring under a wide-open throttle. A few seconds more and it would be out of leaping range. He flung himself off the wall towards it, but again the movement lacked precision. The best he could manage was to grasp the rope rail and hang on, his body and legs dangling.

A man on deck shouted and peered down. Jim had the merest glimpse of his face and the glint of a gold Saint Nicholas medallion on a chain round a thick neck. The man shouted again, urgently: a Scots accent. The vessel swung sharply, deliberately, towards the stone wall. There was no time to do anything. Jim heard as well as felt the crunch of his leg between the metal hull and the stone. He heard himself scream. And that was all.

The boat was well clear by the time the squad got there. There was no immediate sign of Bergerac. A uniformed man looked down from the edge and saw him, afloat but unmoving. Pausing only to drag off his boots, he jumped.

They dashed Jim Bergerac to the hospital in the squad car. A detective constable stayed behind to drive the other car out of the shadows and back to headquarters.

As he got in he noticed something gleaming on the passenger seat. He knew what it was. He picked it up, got out of the car again, and walked back to the harbour edge. He glanced right and left, then drew back his arm and lobbed the whisky bottle as far out as he could send it.

Chapter Two

The first morning British Airways jet from Heathrow was ten minutes late and full. By the time the last passenger had been handed his plastic cup of coffee and packet of biscuits the stewardesses had almost begun collecting the debris from the first-served.

The serried ranks were predominantly male, dark-suited and trim. Many of them worked at documents or read the *Financial Times*. Few troubled to glance out of the windows. It is not for nothing that doorposts of countless St Helier door surrounds bear more nameplates than could be found on any Soho premises. But in place of 'Jacqueline', 'Inge', 'Miss Whipcord' and 'Dusky Masseuse' are the names of corporations, companies, proprietaries, consortia, banks, many of them world-recognised, as well as many others unknown outside the island of Jersey.

There is nothing furtive about the businessmen who enter these premises – not the majority of them, at any rate. They are not looking for relaxation or to indulge fantasies. They are on their mettle, brisk and alert, realists, materialists, traders in figures which owe nothing to voluptuousness, their intercourse conducted over desk tops rather than on couches, their artificial aids the Japanese-made calculator and microchip dictating machine.

This early flight is the one on which some more sensitive tourists feel they are intruding. None of the jolly expectancy of the chartered flights which the tour operators compete to fill. Little striking up of idle chat. Just a red, white and blue vacuum tube transporting a cargo of serious minds the hundred or so miles from southern England to the most southerly of the Channel Islands.

A few nonconformists were on this particular flight,

however. Two were a middle-aged man and wife who held hands nervously at take-off and took more interest than the others in the view once they were airborne, though without sign of excitement.

In the aisle seat beside them sat another man who did not wear the uniform of the business type, but a grey tweed jacket, check shirt and cord slacks.

He would be in his thirties, with dark hair and pale blue eyes, heavy-lidded and almost sleepy-looking, with lines at their corners which gave an impression that he was a ready smiler. His nose was straight and his profile almost Roman. Roman coins, weapons and artefacts have been found on Jersey, although it is not certain that the Islands were actually occupied by them. If Jim Bergerac could have traced his ancestry back a couple of thousand years he might well have found a Roman sailor, or soldier, or trader.

The stewardess arrived with her trolley beside him. His neighbours thanked him for passing her their empty cups. He handed her his own, returning the packet of biscuits unopened.

'Nice to see you again, sir,' she said. She had been too busy earlier to stop for a word. 'Quite some weeks, isn't it?'

'You've got a good memory.'

'We were flying the other way last time,' she reminded him. 'You chatted me up.'

The lines beside his eyes came alive as he remembered and grinned.

'You sat beside me for landing. No point in wasting an opportunity.'

It was her turn to be gratified. 'You actually do remember me?'

'Of course. And you noticed my crutches – but you tactfully didn't mention them.'

She glanced automatically at the long legs, stretched and crossed at the ankles.

'Got rid of them for good, have you?'

He nodded. She smiled and pushed the trolley on.

The exchange of memories carried Jim back some months. After a long spell in hospital on the Island he had been transferred to England, to an establishment in Buckinghamshire specialising in remedial treatment for members of the British armed services, police and others badly injured on public duty. There had been no cosseting there. Relentless exercising was the basis of the therapy, together with acupuncture, which played a more prominent part than would normally have been found inside the public health sector. Jim had looked apprehensively at the tray of fine gold needles and clenched his teeth in anticipation of the first insertion into the back of his crushed leg. To his surprise it had felt no worse than a pin prick, and by the time the area had come to resemble a pincushion he was already feeling drowsy. After five minutes' treatment he had hobbled back to the sun verandah on his aluminium elbow crutches and fallen asleep in mid-conversation with a fellow patient.

But even the inexplicable miracle of acupuncture could not mend in days or weeks unstable fractures, severed tendons and nerves clearly beyond repair. It had been a long slog, much of it under the supervision of merciless men who conducted exercise sessions as though they were punishment, knowing that if their victims cursed them now they would be grateful later.

Jim Bergerac was grateful. He had walked to the aircraft bringing him home without a trace of a limp. He could have sprinted, if necessary. They had restored his crushed limb to seemingly total normality. And they had done more than that. They had dried him out.

Self-pity had never been one of his traits. Self-blame had, though. He had cursed again and again the carelessness which had brought him his injury, and the weakness which had led to that. He had been increasingly on the bottle, heavily in private, less so on duty, but getting worse. Some of his colleagues knew. It was only a matter of time before word got to the top. He had been trying desperately to reclaim himself; but the day of the planned swoop on the drug smugglers had found him at his lowest ebb.

It had been preceded by a night of abuse hurled to and fro between Deborah and himself, fuelled with drink and leaving little time for sleep. He had gone on duty with a thudding hangover and visited a bar at lunchtime to try to rid himself of it by traditional means. That had done him no good. By nightfall he was well-oiled, but dared not admit to unfitness to go on watch. His ultimate mistake had been to take a bottle with him in the car; and as he passed the long waiting hours, brooding on the mess his marriage had become and what it was doing to him, he had drunk far more than he had meant to. When the time to act came he had been half-shot, reflexes dulled, sight and judgment blurred. The smugglers had been clever, and he probably could not have stopped them even if he had been cold sober; but he would not have come near to making himself a permanent cripple in trying.

The cabin announcement bell pinged and the stewardess's voice sounded: 'Ladies and gentlemen, we will shortly be landing at Jersey International Airport . . .'

The aircraft was sinking flatly, its engines changing pitch for the approach.

' . . . Please observe the No Smoking signs and fasten your seat belts, making sure that the back of your seat is in the upright position . . .'

Jim was aware that the man next to him was fumbling unaccustomedly with the harness. He helped him sort it out and watched him supervise his wife in turn. He noticed their glance at one another at the thud of the undercarriage being lowered, and saw them clasp hands again.

The port wing dipped steeply and the Island angled into full view. There were blue blobs everywhere, the swimming pools by the houses of the rich. But the green terrain was amazingly uncluttered for an island no more than nine miles long by five wide, inhabited by some sixty thousand residents, swelled by thousands of tourists. He heard the woman remark something of the sort to her husband.

'Most of the population's in St Helier,' Jim told them. 'Over half. There and amongst the other resorts.'

'Fancy!'

11

They were in level flight again, dropping gently towards the runway.

'Your first visit?'

'That's right.'

'Holiday?'

'No. We . . .'

The man's explanation broke off abruptly. The twin jets had burst into an almost frantic whine and roar. The nose lifted and the aircraft surged upwards again.

The couple's knuckles went white as their grasp tightened.

Jim leaned across them to look down, hastening to reassure them. 'Going to make another circuit.' It was his own first experience of an emergency overshoot and his stomach had lurched with everyone else's, even the blasé businessmen's.

He got a few seconds' glimpse of a side runway. A light aircraft was on it, moving in a weaving sort of way. Heading towards it, as if to catch it or cut it off, was a white van. The wing lifted, and they were lost to his sight.

The captain's voice spoke to them this time, calm and matter-of-fact. 'We do apologise, ladies and gentlemen. Due to unforeseen movement on the ground the aircraft will have to make a second approach to Jersey Airport.'

They turned gradually three hundred and sixty degrees, the green island visible again below. Jim caught sight of a small white plane in flight. He could not tell whether it was the one he had seen on the runway.

The undercarriage clunked down once more and again they settled into a gradual approach, fields and hedges, lanes and cattle coming closer. There was no more conversation. They were almost at ground level. Yellow beacons and markers flashed by, and grass gave way to macadam. The wheels touched and gripped and the jets howled again as the pilot applied reverse thrust, pushing the passengers against their seat backs with the sudden deceleration.

As they sped along, the brakes taking firm hold, Jim saw unusual activity. A fire appliance was speeding out, blue lights flashing urgently. A white police Land Rover was

12

ahead of it, going almost as fast as the taxiing aircraft, an ambulance close behind it. The jet rolled to a halt and they shot by.

Craning her neck at the window, Jim's woman neighbour reported, 'It's something on fire. I think it's a car. Yes. They've got foam hoses going.'

The jet wheeled towards the airport buildings. Looking across the aisle, Jim could see the flames through the opposite windows, a fierce, orange-yellow pyre, round which bobbed the yellow helmets and leggings of firemen and the red and white chequered hats of policemen. Then the scene was out of his sight.

Disobeying the regulation, Jim unclipped his belt while they were still rolling and got up. He grabbed his valise from under the seat in front of his own, and with a farewell nod to the couple got out into the aisle, to move towards the door. His stewardess friend frowned, but before she could remonstrate the aircraft had halted.

'Sorry,' he said. 'Want to be first off.'

'You really have been missing the old place,' she smiled, but the smile he returned her was an impatient courtesy. As soon as the steps were in place and the door opened he hurried out.

The scene of drama was several hundred yards down the runway. Jim spotted an aircraft towing-truck close by, the driver standing in his seat to see what was going on. He hurried across and spoke to the man, identifying himself. The driver nodded. Jim got in and was driven smartly towards the action.

When he jumped down and approached, a young constable he didn't recognise moved swiftly to bar his way; but an airport sergeant was nearby and came up.

'Jim! Didn't know you were back.'

'What the hell's it about?'

'Some crazy fool stealing a plane. Could've been a major disaster with that British Airways jet coming in.'

Amongst the flames and smoke Jim had seen that the wrecked vehicle, lying on its side, was a police van. Not an

13

airport one, either. The ambulance men where shutting their vehicle's back doors. They raced to their cab and drove off at top speed, the siren blaring its double note.

'Are you on this, too?' the sergeant was asking Jim.

'Me? No. I was on the jet. Smart pilot, thank God. What happened?'

The sergeant was staring at him, grim-faced.

'It was one of your lot,' he answered. 'Must have been chasing the nutter. Tried to stop him with the van. Skidded and turned over. Plane got away.'

'Who? Which of my lot?'

'Tom Draycott.'

As the sergeant spoke the name, Jim Bergerac's face hardened. The two detectives had been close, as a working team and as friends.

'Glad to see you've recovered, Jim.'

'I'm OK. Look, I'm going to grab a hire car. Tell whoever gets here from the squad I'm on my way to the hospital.'

He got back on to the towing-truck and was driven off to the airport buildings.

No formalities delayed him. There are few for entry into Jersey anyway, but there was a line of people at the desk. He bypassed them, collecting a few frowns but only a nod from the officer on duty. An advantage – though it could be a disadvantage, too – of being a policeman in a compact community was that one is easily recognised. The official had heard the sirens and had had some word of what was happening. Jim's grim look as he pushed through spoke for itself.

It was the same at the car hire office. Within minutes of leaving the accident scene he was speeding along the main road towards St Helier, ignoring the island's forty mph top limit but watching out carefully for Continental tourists careless of the left-hand rule of the road in this British territory.

As he drove, the car radio gave him the first report of the incident. It told him nothing extra.

Welcome back! Patched up, dried out, divorced now – at the cost of loss of custody of the daughter he loved. Impatient to put together the pieces of his life and career and see what fresh pattern he could make of them. If that airline pilot's reactions had been a fraction slower there might well have been no life left to reassemble.

By the time he got to the hospital Tom Draycott was dead.

Bienvenu, indeed.

Chapter Three

Young women engaged on police work do not cry easily. Not on duty, at least; in private life it may be different.

Charlotte Duvalier was on duty, and she was crying. She was trying her best to hide it by bending her head over the filing cabinet's open drawer. Detective Inspector Barney Crozier was not a particularly astute man, having only recently attained his rank after a slow plod, but as he entered the office he needed no more than a glance at the plump bureau secretary's twitching shoulders to recognise her state. He made no concession to it.

'Any news from Air Traffic?'

She didn't turn round and her answer was muffled. 'Nothing yet.'

'The plane's owner?'

'Not been able to contact him. They think he may be abroad.'

Crozier left her to it, returning to his own office adjoining: an unhandsome though not ugly man in his mid-thirties, whose set features, prematurely lined forehead and receding hairline bore witness to his perpetual state of concern that he was acting precisely as the rule books instructed. Had he ignored them sometimes and leap-frogged regulations, gambling that a successful outcome would disarm possible criticism, he might have made Inspector several years before this and already been well on towards Detective Chief Inspector.

The offices were in a Georgian building at one end of St Helier's Royal Square, presided over by the gilt statue of King George the Second wearing a toga. In the area reserved for parking police vehicles Jim Bergerac was at that moment locking the door of the hire car and being hailed by a CID

16

man. They shook hands, but their exchange of greetings was sobered by the shock of their colleague's violent death.

'It's ironic,' Jim voiced what he had been thinking. 'If my flight hadn't been ten minutes late I might have been on hand to help poor Tom. He mightn't have died.'

'Lucky you didn't die yourself and everyone else in that jet.'

'There's that. Any idea who's handling this case, Sid?'

'Inspector Crozier.'

'*Inspector?*'

'Made up while you've been away.'

Another part in the reassembly pattern. Jim was several years Barney Crozier's junior, but he had had reason to believe he would make Inspector first. That disastrous evening had cost him even more than he'd realised; or perhaps his drinking had already been in the files.

'There've been other changes,' the CID man went on. 'New department. *Bureau des Étrangers.*'

'*Bureau des* what?'

'Anything to do with outsiders.'

'Tourists and businessmen?'

'Them and anyone else not native to the island. Conference visitors, foreign labour, immigrant settlers. Even our big-name tax exiles and millionaires – like your father-in-law.'

'*Ex*-father-in-law,' Jim corrected him. 'Divorce came through while I was away.'

'Sorry.'

'No need. Only good news in six months.'

'Well, it's good news you're back. Fully mobile?'

'Not even a limp,' Jim demonstrated as they walked into the building. He automatically turned to accompany the other towards the CID squad offices, but Sid jerked his thumb in the opposite direction.

'If you want Barney, he's head of the new bureau. Tom Draycott was on attachment to it. Down the end there.'

Charlotte raised her puffy eyes momentarily as the office door opened. At the sight of Jim she smiled, despite the tears.

She, too, had been a CID secretary until Crozier had brought her to the new department with him. She was in her twenties and pretty. Jim had never seen her crying before. Her normal state was the good humour which seems to go with plumpness.

They exchanged a few words, enabling Charlotte to overcome her tears. Jim knew they were for Tom. She had had an almost sisterly relationship with both men, closer than with Crozier, who regarded a secretary as just that.

The sound of Jim's voice brought Crozier out. They shook hands.

'Congratulations, Barney,' said Jim ungrudgingly.

'Thanks. Come on through.'

He waved Jim ahead of him into his office, himself holding back a moment to catch Charlotte's eye and point to a name at the head of a list of internal telephone extensions on the wall behind her desk. He nodded towards it, and she understood.

Barney Crozier's office was small, square, and low ceilinged, like most of the others in the building. It was uncluttered, neatly functional, its only decorations a number of framed photographs of Jersey policemen of the 'twenties and 'thirties, grouped on and around motorcycles which today's collectors of vintage machines would covet.

Crozier took his proprietorial place behind his desk. Jim felt too impatient to sit down.

'I want to work on this one with you, Barney,' he said without preamble.

Crozier looked at him levelly. 'Have to see the Chief first, Jim. You belong to the squad.'

'They've done without me long enough. What was Tom working on?'

'He had one or two routine jobs in hand. Nothing that should have led him to the airport and that crazy chase.'

'Who was he after?'

'We don't know. He was haphazard – like you, Jim. Bit of one enquiry here, bit of another there. Too fond of solo work without keeping people posted. You should have stayed at the airport as a witness, you know.'

'I was just a passenger. I only saw what the rest did.'

'And barging into the hospital was hardly correct form.'

'For God's sake Barney! Tom was my friend.'

They were interrupted by Charlotte coming in. Her eyes were still red, but she was calm now. She said to Jim, 'Excuse me. The Chief wants to see you straight away.'

Jim moved to the door, telling Crozier as he went, 'You'd better start clearing a desk for me.'

Crozier made no reply; only watched him go, looking for the limp which wasn't there.

The Chief of the Jersey States Police is the equivalent of a Chief Constable on the mainland. He is the man answerable to the Defence Committee, one of half-a-dozen committees which administer the Island. Jersey has its own government, code of laws and judicial body, the Royal Court. The Chief's job is no sinecure on a tiny, sun-drenched island which is the envy of its visitors for its beauty, its natural amenities, its low cost of living, low income tax and complete absence of such tiresome impositions as VAT or Death and Estate Duties. Great wealth is present, both in visible terms of property and possessions and in the less tangible form of digits in the computers and ledgers of the thousands of companies which use Jersey as an offshore base and bourse for their transactions. Wealth, tangible or intangible, is a focus and magnet for crime; and while violence, social unrest and the other forms of trouble which have transformed life in Britain for the worse inside little more than a decade do not much occupy the Jersey States Police, there is plenty more to concern them, not least the fact that, with its centuries-old connection with smuggling, the island is sometimes used as a staging post for the movement of drugs between North Africa, the Continent and England.

The Chief, who did Jim the courtesy of getting up to come from behind his big desk to shake hands warmly, was tall and strongly built, very fit in his fifties. He was formally dressed in a blue pin-striped business suit. His eyes were smiling but shrewdly observant, and when he spoke his mild Lancashire

19

accent could not be missed. He had come up from young constable on the beat in the Lancashire Constabulary, via Scotland Yard, to this supreme office which he had held for five years now and would, he could confidently anticipate, see him through the rest of his career.

'Really good to see you, Jim,' he said, meaning it, in spite of all that he knew.

'And you, Chief. You've lost weight.'

The Chief patted his flat stomach. 'Over a stone since I changed my tailor. But you're the one with the healthy glow.'

'It's been a healthy spell.'

The Chief waved him into a chair and went back to his own.

'I hear they work their patients hard.'

'Tougher than any police college.'

'Well, it obviously works. Care for a drink?'

There was no change in the friendly expression to reveal that the question was less casually asked than it appeared. Jim shook his head. 'No thanks. I've lost the habit.'

It made the Chief feel a little better to hear this confirmation of what the reports had told him. But there was still the rest of their contents. He drew a file nearer to him, but didn't open it at once. He raised his eyes to meet Jim's frankly.

'Jim . . . I'm afraid I have some bad news.'

'I know. I saw it happen, just as I was landing.'

'Tom Draycott. Tragic, yes. But I don't mean that. It concerns you. Your re-employment.'

He picked up his reading glasses and put them on, opening the file.

'Your latest medical report was forwarded a week ago. Of course, you'll be checked by our own board . . .'

'They told me that.'

' . . . but the Police Surgeon's gone over the file already. It says you aren't fit enough to stay with the Force.'

If Jim hadn't been sitting he would have swayed at the shock. The Chief was looking at him again, his expression almost wretched.

20

'They leave this sort of dirty work to people like me. Apparently, in spite of all the effort – theirs and yours – your medical grade remains far below police requirements. Unstable fractures, severed tendons, certain nerves beyond repair . . .'

'Do I look like a cripple?' Jim erupted. 'Have I even a bloody limp?'

The Chief pointed to the file. There was no triumph in the gesture. 'They sent the X-rays.' He read from one document: '"The patient displays outstanding powers of will to subjugate the pain his injuries must still cause him, even enabling him to adopt a posture suggesting total fitness." In other words, they admire your guts, but you can't fool them.'

Jim spared this kindly man none of the bitterness he was feeling. 'You promised me my job back. You're telling me I can't have it.'

'I'm truly sorry, Jim.'

'That's what the Met. said to that boy who had his hand blown off. And his Commissioner had told him not to worry about a thing.'

'I know. But you'd be a risk to others as well as yourself.'

'You've just lost a copper. Aren't we in the business of taking risks?'

The Chief got up and went to stare out of the window.

'I know it's a terrible blow. I have to go by what the doctors say. The Senator and the Defence Committee concur.'

'Do they concur over your ulcer, that would double you up if you weren't as tough as blazes?' Jim, too, was standing now. The Chief turned to him, as he demanded, 'You sure it wasn't the booze influenced them? I told you, that's under control.'

'It had nothing to do with it. Jim, you aren't making this easy for me . . .'

'How the hell do I, when you give me the chop? I suppose you expect me to walk out with a smile, carrying my head under my arm!'

'I could fix you up with a civvie job.'

'No, Chief. I'll appeal, through the Federation.'

The Chief sighed, relieved to have got over the most distasteful part.

'That's your right, of course. Until then you remain on sick leave and full pay. Believe me, I'm truly sorry.'

Jim knew he was speaking the truth.

'Forget it. You had to do it.'

He nodded and went out, leaving the door open. Inspector Crozier came in almost immediately.

'How did he take it?' he asked the Chief.

'How d'you think? Poor bastard. And he thought he'd touched rock bottom and come back up. If you want my job, Barney, let me know.'

Chapter Four

Jim left the building without pausing to talk to anyone. He suddenly felt they all knew; that all he would get would be falsely hearty greetings and tactful evasions. He noticed Charlotte glance at him as he passed through the outer office. She was no longer crying, but looked deeply sorrowful. He wondered if any of her pity was for him. He could have managed a few tears of his own.

He went out into Royal Square, wondering how many eyes were watching him from the police building's windows, hoping to detect the limp that would salve their consciences a bit. He walked deliberately briskly, heading for the long pedestrian-only shopping thoroughfare where the main banks have branches. He went into his own, drew some money, and then made for the Central Market, a stylish 1880s construction of red-painted ironwork roofed with thousands of panes of glass, supported by forty tall granite pillars, with an elaborately ornamented fountain in the middle of its spacious concourse. The scent of massed flowers and produce as he entered lifted his spirits momentarily. It was good, too, to hear again the ancient island patois, derived from Norman French, being bandied amongst the stallholders. Several of them recognised him and waved or called out. He responded with a show of cheerfulness, but didn't pause to talk to any of them.

His objective was a booth bearing a large sign AUX VINS DE FRANCE. Row upon row of bottles of wines and spirits of every variety occupied its windows and walls, to stagger tourists by their incredibly low prices and tempt even tee-totallers to accept a bargain. Jim drew out his wallet; but it was not a bottle he bought. The store also sold cigarettes, tobacco, cigars, and confectionery. The last of these was

23

what he was after. He chose a basket of sweets, daintily decorated with pink ribbon bows.

Carrying it unwrapped but without embarrassment, he returned to Royal Square again and got into the hire car. He glanced at his watch and drove out of town northward to the parish of St Mary, reaching one of the inland villages just in time to see neatly uniformed children emerging from a white and blue painted stone building bearing a name plaque ÉCOLE ÉLÉMENTAIRE 1901.

Several mothers with cars were waiting for their children. There were one or two larger vehicles, their uniformed chauffeurs chatting together. Parked a little away from the rest was a chocolate brown Rolls-Royce, its chauffeur behind the wheel. Jim pulled up nearby and went across. The chauffeur knew him but greeted him warily. Jim explained himself and gestured towards the children. The chauffeur shrugged, nodded, and drove the Rolls away.

Jim turned towards the trickle of children, just in time to see the one he was looking for: a girl of ten, pretty and trim in maroon jumper, black skirt and white stockings below the knee.

'Kim!'

'Daddy!'

She was in his arms and he was lifting her off the ground, swinging her round in the shared delight of reunion.

'I sent the Rolls home,' he told her. 'I'll take you myself.'

'Have they made you better, Daddy? Really?'

'Fit as a fiddle.'

'You won't have to go away again?'

He shook his head. He didn't know how much she had been told, or understood. It was why he had hoped to get a little time alone with her, so that he would know where he stood.

In the car he presented her with the basket of sweets. She started on them without ceremony, putting one into his mouth for him as he drove.

'When you've changed out of your school things I thought we'd go to the zoo,' he told her, speaking around the sugary sweet. 'Or Corbière lighthouse.'

'Mmm. Have to ask Mummy, though.'

'I don't think she'll object.'

'I know you're divorced now.'

He hadn't expected it to come out quite so directly.

'Oh, do you?'

'Mummy told me, last time we came back from seeing you in hospital.'

'Well, no point in keeping secrets between us all, is there?'

'You don't love her any more, do you?'

Had he ever – really? 'I love you,' he compromised.

'She sold the cottage,' Kim said, rummaging amongst the sweets for another pink one. 'I don't like it so much at Grandad's.'

'You've got your own pony, though, I hear.'

'Yes. Sir Walter. After Sir Walter Raleigh. He used to be Governor of Jersey, you know.'

'So he did. So, a titled pony, eh.'

'Grandad says it's more than he's got – a title.'

He would say that, Jim thought, and mean it. Still, bigger crooks than he had posed outside Buckingham Palace gates.

'Mummy has a boy friend,' came the next jolting piece of information. 'He takes her sailing. He's called Jeremy.'

'Has he a title?'

'No. But I heard her tell Grandad he's very rich.'

That would be a prerequisite this time round. Millionaire's daughter and detective sergeant hadn't been the ideal mix.

They had reached the coast. The twinkling blue sea was below them. He turned the car into the curving driveway of a whitewashed Georgian mansion in immaculate grounds with palm trees and scissor-trimmed lawn in the foreground. The brown Rolls stood outside a garage converted from a large stable.

Residential property is hard to buy or lease. Open the gates freely to well-off mainlanders and foreigners and the locals would soon be priced out. The agricultural acreage which, with tourism, maintains the economy, is safeguarded from development. Thus, only Jersey-born people with at least ten years' total residence can buy or lease without restriction. There are other degrees of entitlement, forfeited after three months' absence at a stretch.

Another regulation reads: 'Newcomers require the specific consent of the Housing Department before any property may be bought or rented. Consent will normally only be granted where the applicant can satisfy the Department that they will be of economic or social benefit to the Island . . . In any case, newcomers granted a specific consent are required to take up units of accommodation in least demand by local persons.'

That was a fair description of Charlie Hungerford's mansion, parkland acres, stables and paddocks, tennis court, swimming pool, etcetera. There are perhaps sixty millionaires in the Island, a ratio of more than one to the square mile. Some are self-exiled from rundown old Britain. A handful are the very, very rich: mysterious, seldom glimpsed, deliberately maintaining a low profile behind secure defences, and a staff of off-putting aides and domestics. There is not, on the whole, much demand from local persons for the kind of property either of these categories inhabits.

Exactly how Charlie Hungerford had satisfied the official requirements that he should be of economic or social benefit to the Island Jim Bergerac had never been told, nor tried to find out. This particular millionaire was now aged sixty, still kept up his Yorkshire bluntness and the accent which went with it, still took a pride in getting his hands dirty from labour on his estate, then dressing in expensively cut tweed and flannel to drive into St Helier for meetings of diverse boards and committees, or nip across on a direct flight to Leeds, where the heart of his business enterprises pumped steady profits into his many Jersey bank accounts.

Jim supposed that officialdom had different yardsticks than his by which to measure a man's suitability. Hard businessmen had a way of getting what they wanted, even at the cost of one or two initial turndowns. Charlie was the persevering sort: tough, determined, and, Jim knew, dishonest if it paid to be and could be covered up. That was how he regarded the man who, for ten increasingly uncomfortable years, had been his father-in-law.

As Jim pulled up the car on the drive, and Kim scrambled impatiently out, the front door opened and Deborah came out. Deborah Bergerac, *née* Hungerford. The ex-Mrs Bergerac. Thirty, blonde, slim, cold to the touch, and with a heart as hard as the first-grade pearls she wore over her twin set.

It was no welcoming gesture, merely a coincidence. She was wheeling behind her a golf cart and bag of clubs. She stared at Jim without a smile, and promptly shook her head at a question from Kim, who had run to her.

'You know you're expected at Lucy Corlett's for tea. Hurry up and change. We're late as it is.'

Kim turned to her father. He shrugged. 'We'll make it tomorrow, darling. *If* that's convenient.'

She went disappointedly into the house.

'I wanted to give her a treat,' he explained, following Deborah to the Rolls. She lifted the big boot and placed the golf things in.

'You should have phoned,' she told him. 'The Corletts live next to the course. It's handy.'

'Golfing while they throw buns about? Well, how are you, Deborah?'

'I'm fine, thank you. And you?' She looked pointedly towards his leg.

'Never better. You settling down okay?'

'What do you mean "settling down"? This is my home. I never wanted to leave it.'

'So you've been known to remark. I hear you managed to sell the cottage.'

'First viewer. Your share's in your bank. Your things are in the garage, with your old car.'

She closed the boot and went dismissively into the house. He heard her calling sharply to Kim to hurry up.

There was no point in going in. He went instead to the stable garage and opened the door. Amongst boxes and suitcases and with its own open seats and boot crammed with his belongings waited his faithful friend, a maroon Triumph Roadster, early nineteen-fifties vintage. He was pleased to see it again, second only to his daughter.

He wandered round it, admiring its line and condition as if it were a thoroughbred stallion. A Yorkshire accent said, behind him, 'Pity you never looked at my daughter that way, Jim.'

He turned to see Charlie Hungerford, tall, slim, boiler-suited and with grizzled hair showing under the sides of his hard white helmet. He was grimy and grinning. They didn't shake hands.

'Hello, Charlie,' Jim said. 'What is it today? Excavating a second swimming pool?'

'Fall-out shelter. Everybody should have one.'

'For the man who's got everything.'

'You could have had, or some of it, if you'd played it my way.'

'A cop go into partnership with a bent scrap dealer?'

Hungerford went on grinning, but the blades they crossed in verbal thrusts and parries were always sharp-edged.

'Demolition, Jim. Demolition and scrap. A business running itself across the Channel, legitimately. I worked for everything I've got. I was driving excavators when you were playing with your first toy handcuffs.'

'Yeah. I guess I did have a vocation.'

'You think it's a crime to be rich. Well it's not. Anybody else would've crossed the great divide. You wouldn't, and what did you get – your leg mangled and lost Deborah.'

If he had added 'and Kim' Jim might have found it hard not to hit him.

'Take it easy, Charlie,' he said instead.

The older man nodded. 'All right. And you. I heard the news about that Draycott at the airport. Didn't you bring him here once?'

'Kim's christening.'

'Too bad, that. You on the case?'

'Assisting.'

'So here you are, then. Return to go.'

'Right.'

'Where'll you be living?'

'I'll let you know. I'll tell the hire people to collect their car.'

28

'Suit yourself. Welcome back, Jim.'

Charlie turned and walked away, leaving Jim in the garage to sort through his belongings, choosing which to keep in the Triumph.

Yes, a piece of all that was Charlie Hungerford's lifestyle could have been his for the agreeing. He hadn't even considered it. Deborah's urging and his repeated refusals had fanned their smouldering hostility into flame and ultimate conflagration. His only fear had been how badly Kim might have got singed. Not severely, it seemed.

He really had owned some tin handcuffs as a little boy. Once, he had got them snapped fast on both his wrists and been unable to free himself. He had cried and his mother had had to rescue him.

He had handcuffed himself to Deborah, but was now released again. He had handcuffed himself to a career as a policeman, and regarded the key as thrown away. It seemed they had found it, and were determined to use it.

The Triumph's tyres were hard enough and there was petrol in the tank. She started second go. He drove out of the opulent driveway, but instead of heading back towards the coast he meandered along narrow country lanes, letting the car take him where it wished between fields of greenhouses, potato plantations, pastures where creamy-coloured Jersey cattle stood or lay, tethered individually, contentedly chewing, turning soft eyes to see him pass. He passed warm red granite houses, chapels, pubs, walls, gardens, cultivated terraces. The smell of seaweed, used to fertilise the land, reached him pleasantly in the open car.

The shock of the tragedy which had been his first homecoming experience, together with the bitterness of finding the Force wanted to dispense with him and that his ex-wife would clearly prefer him to go away and relinquish any claim to their daughter, began to recede. However people regarded him, he could feel that the Island itself was welcoming him back; and that mattered most.

Chapter Five

The question of where he would live would have to wait while he sorted everything out. If the Force ditched him he might even have to leave the Island. It was all the more incentive to hang on.

The more immediate requirement, a place to stay, was easily met. He drove that evening to St Aubin, across the bay from St Helier, and looked up Diamanté Lil.

Her real name was so ordinary that it only appeared on official documents and made her shudder when she saw it. To everyone outside the bureaucracies she was Lil, Diamanté for her trademarks of glittering earrings, necklace, many bracelets, and the comb in her brassy hair. She had once been a dancer and still had the curves, even if the flesh was no longer quite prime cut. But her personality scintillated like her ornaments and was one of the reasons for the popularity of the Royal Barge bar and shellfish restaurant on the St Aubin waterfront. She owned it in partnership with the chef, known to everyone simply by his first name, Gulliver, whose cooking was the other reason why the Royal Barge was in the top league on an island abounding with excellent places to eat.

Jim recognised several regular patrons as he entered, relieved to find no change in the surroundings, with the French-style zinc-topped bar, the familiar chequered tablecloths, the smell of garlic cookery, and, above all, Lil herself, with a laugh as loud as her jewellery, serving a couple at the far end of the bar.

She saw him and gave a welcoming shriek: 'No! I don't believe it. It's a ghost!'

She deserted the customers, hurrying from behind the bar. 'A ghost? Do I look that bad?' he said.

She gave him a great hug and kiss, evoking a few cheers and 'Bravos!'

The door from the kitchen opened as Gulliver came out to see what the noise was for, still carrying a long carving knife. He was a small Westcountryman, whose comical expression and heavy-rimmed spectacles gave him so close a resemblance to Eric Morecambe that cries of 'What do you think of it so far?' 'Rubbish!' were often bandied between the higher-spirited regulars when he did the rounds to ask if they were enjoying the food. He took it as affectionately complimentary, as it was invariably meant.

What his relationship with Diamanté Lil was, other than as co-proprietor, and even how that had come about, no one knew. Her seemingly infinite warmth for all her friends perhaps reached its highest temperature when she was alone with the little man, who played up to her like a comedienne's feed.

'Oh-ho, caught in the act!' he cried, raising the knife, to further cheers. Then he laid it on the bar, to shake Jim's hand warmly with both his own, and the rest of the company went back to minding its own business.

'This calls for a real celebration,' Lil was enthusing, getting champagne glasses for the three of them. But Jim shook his head, although a trifle wistfully.

'Not for me, Lil, thanks. Orange juice or a tonic will do.'

'If It's a hangover I know just the thing.'

'I'm off it. Alcoholics Anonymous. The lot.'

'Well, there goes half our profits.' Lil made a face at Gulliver, who grinned, clapped Jim on the arm, and went back to his kitchen.

'Seriously, Jim?'

'For good – I hope. All I want, Lil, is a room for a few days. Can you manage it?' Jim knew that a couple of rooms were kept made up for the benefit of the odd patron who had lingered too long, or drunk too deeply, to catch his plane back to England or the hydrofoil to St Malo. He had slept there a time or two himself when he couldn't face going back to the cottage and the abuse he had known was awaiting him from Deborah.

"'Course, love,' Lil said. 'You know that.'

'Thanks.'

He would have chatted on with her, but, across the room, he had caught sight of Barney Crozier. He was sitting at the 'reading table', a long shelf broad enough to accommodate glasses and snack plates, with the day's newspapers affixed vertically above, like sheets of music on a piano. Crozier had a drink and a sandwich before him, and Jim could see that the local evening newspaper he was studying carried a front-page headline and photograph of the airport drama. He excused himself to Lil and went over.

'We any further ahead than the reporters?' he asked.

Crozier looked up with a frown. 'Not much.'

'So the mystery man got clean away, did he?'

'Unless he's at the bottom of the sea.'

'Might have been a local villain with flying experience. What about Island robberies lately?'

The reply carried clear resentment at this interference. It would not have been Barney Crozier's style when they had both been sergeants. 'He stole that plane. We've traced the owner – away in Australia, buying sheep. Perfectly straight.'

'Maybe he was driving to the airport to catch a scheduled flight. Spotted Tom Draycott was on to him and panicked.'

Crozier wiped the sandwich crumbs from his fingers with the paper serviette and drank the last inch of his pale beer. He got up.

'If there's any news, you'll read about it – Sergeant.'

It stung. Jim managed a rueful smile, nevertheless.

'Barney, you wouldn't pull rank on me?'

'What rank? From now on, I gather, yours is virtually a courtesy title.'

The Inspector walked on and out of the bar.

Jim ate his first gourmet meal for months that evening. He had promised himself it for long enough, but found he couldn't enjoy it. The seafood wasn't the same with only Perrier water to accompany it; and the bitter experiences of the day had soured his gastric juices. He ate it all, so as not to offend Gulliver, and when Lil insisted it was on the house he didn't argue, for the same reason.

He spent the next day attending to personal affairs in St Helier and did not go into HQ. The hell with them. If they insisted he was still on sick leave they could send for him when, and if, they wanted him.

The newspaper told him that Tom Draycott's funeral would be the following afternoon. He was not letting them inhibit him from being there. He bought a small flowered wreath, writing simply 'Jim' on the card.

He put it with the others which were awaiting placing on the grave. The funeral was at St Brelade's Parish Church, high above the bay where Tom had made himself so expert a water skier. A strong wind blustered through the forest of Victorian headstones and ruffled the bared heads of the men. As well as Tom's family and civilian friends they included several policemen. Crozier stared at Jim as though he were an interloper. The Chief, in uniform and medal ribbons, gave him his sad-eyed nod.

As the burial service was read, Jim couldn't help watching a particular girl who stood alongside Tom's parents. She was small and slender, but her most catching feature was the long jet-black hair which tossed in the wind. She made no attempt to brush it away from her pale face, staring fixedly at the coffin draped with the Jersey police flag, until after the committal, when she turned away before the soil was cast in.

When Jim went to say his condolences to Mr and Mrs Draycott they introduced him to her as Francine Leland, Tom's fiancée.

'He wrote me about you,' he told her, 'but he didn't say you were actually engaged.'

She fingered her ring. 'Only just. He told me of you also. How you were hurt.' Her accent was French but her English almost perfect.

'I was luckier. Where are you from?'

'I'm with the Tourism Office.'

'I mean what place? You're not an Islander.'

'Cherbourg.' She touched the ring again. 'I'd have qual-

33

ified as a Jersey resident if Tom and I had married, but I don't know if I would have been the right choice for him.'

'Why ever not?'

'I was too much afraid I would not have been good as a policeman's wife.'

Jim glanced towards the other policemen. They were out of earshot against the strong wind. He asked her, 'He didn't say anything to you about the case – the one he was on when . . . ?'

'He didn't talk about his cases and I never asked. Inspector Crozier asked me a lot of questions, but there was nothing I could tell him.'

'Nobody should die bravely like that without a reason being found.'

'What difference would it make? It will not bring Tom back.'

She left him abruptly, to rejoin Tom's parents, the wind lifting and dropping the black mourning veil of her hair like a horse's black mane.

Chapter Six

It was calm next morning at Havre de Pas, just beyond where he parked the car, to wander along the front, feeling strangely unoccupied and irresolute. Rows of deckchairs faced the sea, mostly occupied by elderly tourists, dressed in almost every permutation of clothing from flowered beach shirts and shorts to overcoats, their skins angrily pink from unwary exposure to sunlight and ozone. Sunburn is the Island's only indigenous health hazard.

'Hello there,' a man hailed as he paused to lean on the iron railing. He turned, half-expecting the greeting to be meant for someone else. An elderly couple, seated side by side, were smiling at him. He recognised his neighbours in the aircraft.

'Enjoying your holiday?' the man asked.

Jim leaned his back on the railing. 'I'm local. Enjoying yours, I hope?'

The woman answered, sad-faced. 'It's not a holiday for us, either. Our daughter's very ill in hospital. They sent for us.'

'I'm sorry. Was she taken ill?'

'Knocked down by a car. She was working here as an au pair. Nearly killed.'

'Hit-and-run, the police say,' the man said. 'They found the car but not the driver. Don't hold out much hope of getting him.'

'Why not?'

'The officer on the case was that poor lad who got killed at the airport. That fire we saw.'

'Ever so nice he sounded on the telephone,' his wife said. 'Told us he'd meet the plane and take us to the hospital himself.'

Jim was alert suddenly. 'He didn't say any more – any details?'

'No. We went to the police station when we heard it was him had been killed, but they couldn't tell us anything. He hadn't spoken to any of the others, and his notebook got . . . well, burnt up with him.'

'You've been able to see your daughter, though?'

'Oh yes. They took us. They were very nice to us, but there wasn't much else they could do. Mary's out of danger now, so we're going home tomorrow and she'll be able to fly home soon.'

'Mind if I go and see her?'

The couple exchanged surprised glances. 'You'd have to ask the coppers.'

'I'm one of them. Tom Draycott was my best friend.'

Mary Pollender was pretty, under the facial bruises and cuts. The Sister had told him she had multiple fractures. She was still on a drip, but was able to talk easily with him.

'It was my afternoon off. I'd been for a walk and I was just going back down the hill to Rozel Bay. He came round the bend on the wrong side of the road. Took it too wide. Sent me flying. Have you taken over from that dishy-looking fella?'

Jim had been warned by the Sister that they hadn't told her of Tom Draycott's death, for fear of adding to her shock.

'That's right. He didn't get a chance to give me all the details. Mind repeating them?'

'There isn't much, except the bit of description.'

'Description? You were able to see the driver?'

'I wasn't unconscious straightaway. He pulled up and came back to look at me.'

'But he didn't help you?'

'Didn't touch me. Just looked at me and muttered something.'

'You can't remember what?'

'Only the sound. A sort of foreign accent, but not pronounced. Something like "Good God!", but I can't say for sure.'

'And the description?'

'About forty, I think. Red hair. I've remembered since,

though. He had a leather coat on and one of those plastic sort of hats the Yanks wear.'

'You didn't tell Constable Draycott this?'

'I hadn't remembered it till today. I was going to tell him when he comes next.'

'He's . . . off the case, I'm afraid. You say the man just left you there?'

'I heard him drive off before I passed out. They found the car abandoned a long way from there. Sorel Point.'

'Okay, Mary, thanks. I'll keep in touch.'

She gave him a painful smile. 'Next time you see your dishy pal, tell him off for standing me up.'

The smile he returned her, getting up to leave, was every bit as painful to him.

He was able to smile genuinely a few minutes later as he walked thoughtfully away from the hospital and saw Francine Leland. She was standing on the pavement, wearing smart Tourism Office uniform and holding a clipboard. She was talking animatedly with the driver of a luxury coach, who made a final despairing gesture with both hands, slammed the automatic doors shut, and drove off.

'He looks happy,' Jim remarked.

She was pleased to see him. 'We sent him to the airport to meet thirty Japanese delegates to a conference. Don't ask me how, but they flew to Guernsey instead. He's nothing to grumble about. He'll get paid extra for collecting them when they get rescued.'

Jim had a thought. 'What about you? Left high and dry too?'

'Till they arrive, yes.'

'Care to devote your spare time to something else?'

He explained briefly and her expression grew serious.

'But it's only a guess,' she said doubtfully. 'It could have been someone else entirely whom Tom saw at the airport and chased.'

'It could. But there's a chance it was that hit-and-run driver. It was the day after the accident. Maybe Tom reasoned he'd be trying to get away from the Island in a hurry and was keeping his eyes open for him. He never let up on cases.'

'That was one of the reasons I doubted it would work for us. But what do you mean about devoting my time?'

'So far, I'm the only one who knows the man was wearing a leather coat and a funny hat. Odds are he would have got rid of them as quick as possible. I don't know what, if anything, our people found in the abandoned car, but he certainly wouldn't have left those things in it. I'm going to drive to Sorel Point and look round. If you're game, two searchers would be more effective than one.'

'You're as obsessive as Tom, aren't you?'

'Yeah. Fair enough in a cop, but tricky as a human being.'

'Is that why your marriage failed?'

'Partly. It depends a lot on the wife, Francine. Mine was a millionaire's daughter. Not the type at all.'

'I'm called Frankie,' she said. 'Where's your car?'

As they drove northward the stream of her black hair behind her in the open car fascinated him.

He told her more about himself, feeling he could talk freely with this girl who had been going to marry his best friend. Jim's parents, no longer alive now, had been native Islanders. His father built boats, got away ahead of the German occupation to serve in the Royal Navy throughout the war, and returned soon after the liberation of the Islands. One of the first things he did when he got back was to marry the farmer's daughter who had waited for him. Jim was their only child.

He went to elementary school and then a local grammar, on a scholarship. Somehow, not just because of the toy handcuffs, he had always known he wanted to be a policeman. He had been accepted by the local force and sent to the Metropolitan Police College at Hendon. After passing out he was attached to Sussex Constabulary for experience and stationed at Brighton.

'I was there exactly two years,' he told her. 'Deborah was at Sussex University. We met at a party. She was quite a stunner, and she took a shine to me. To cut a sad but familiar story short, I got her, as they say, with child. Or, I

38

sometimes think, she got me with child. At any rate, I was hooked.'

'You didn't want to be?'

'Oh yes. Quite a catch for me too, a millionaire's daughter, great looker, lots of fun – in those days. My dad was dead by then, and I knew how proud Mum would be of me. I wasn't sure whether Deb's old man would be quite so keen, but she talked him into letting us marry. What I didn't realise was that they thought it automatically made me their property – healthy young guy for daughter to cuddle when inclined, and act as social dogsbody on the Island. Ambitious copper, able to pull a few strings, turn blind-eyes on dad's shadier deals, maybe slip him the inside word when appropriate. I only realised that after we were married and I'd come back to duty in Jersey. I told him I wasn't having any.'

'Too late for him to stop you marrying by then.'

'He wasn't pleased. Nor was Deb, once she found out what being a detective's wife was like. The hours, the stress. Not her scene at all. They ganged up to get me to resign and join daddy's company. Seat on the board, that sort of thing. I wouldn't. Maybe it was selfish, but I didn't fancy playing gamekeeper turned poacher. So that's the story. Downhill from there. Rows. Drinking. We'd have split sooner, but for our daughter Kim.'

'These people,' Francine asked, looking at him. 'Do I know them?'

'Probably. Not the Island's most reclusive millionaire, Charlie. Charlie Hungerford.'

'Oh, but of course I know him. I painted his portrait.'

Jim glanced at her, surprised.

'His daughter – your ex-wife – commissioned it for his sixtieth birthday last month. Only she did not say her name was Bergerac.'

'She's gone back to being Hungerford. Clean break department. But I didn't know you were an artist.'

'That's my other life. I got the Tourism job to keep me while I paint, or I would not be allowed to stay. You'd be surprised how many people in Jersey want to have their portraits done.'

'I wouldn't, you know. Above all else they want to go down in posterity, preferably not having paid too much tax for the privilege.'

'If I had known Mr Hungerford was so rich I might have charged a little more.'

'You wouldn't have got it, not from a man who made his brass knocking things down. I don't know who did more damage to England, him or Adolf Hitler.'

They were turning on to the minor road which peters out near Sorel Point. A horn sounded loudly behind them and an American convertible, too big for Island driving, swept past. Its top was down and the driver was the only occupant. She was a black girl, very black, with a skin that shone in the sunlight and swept-up hair. She flashed them a big white friendly grin and waved as she sped by, her radio blaring. There weren't too many black girls in Jersey. She had to be rich, or with somebody who was.

It didn't take them long to find the place where the hit-and-run car had been left. There was only one likely spot on this rocky, precipitous part of the coast. The grass had been crushed by the car's tyres and police boots and a stake had been driven into the sparse soil as a marker. The ground fell away in terraces below. That was where they searched and where, under some wire shrubbery, Jim found the leather coat. Almost simultaneously, working at a slightly higher level, Francine pulled from under a stone a fawn-coloured hat with a plastic covering.

'Well, you were right,' she said, turning the hat in her hands. 'He was afraid to be recognised afterwards, so he hid his things. But the girl he knocked down didn't tell Tom about the clothes. You think he recognised him even without that description?'

'You know, Frankie, you've got a bit of a cop's mind yourself. Either the man Tom was chasing at the airport wasn't this joker, or he was, and Tom knew him in some other connection. Nothing to do with the hit-and-run.'

Chapter Seven

'Charlotte?'

'Yes?'

'Jim Bergerac – only call me Fred if anyone's listening.'

'Hello, Fred. Fancy hearing from you again.'

'Good girl. Do me a favour and I'll buy you a lobster supper.'

'For a lobster supper you get all my favours. What is it?'

'Firstly, any news of that plane?'

Her voice dropped as she held the telephone close to her mouth. He could picture her at her desk in the Bureau, with Crozier's door open near her.

'It's not been found yet, but we've been on to the maintenance engineer. He said there wasn't enough fuel in the tanks to keep it airborne more than about fifteen minutes.'

'Right. Second, can you run a hush-hush check for me with London – Special Branch? Only a description to go on. The man's a white South African, maybe Johannesburg, about forty, red hair, recently visitor to England and the Island, and connections with the arms business. Got it?'

'Right. Where do I get hold of you?'

'I'll call you. About an hour?'

She reverted to her normal voice.

'OK. Nice talking to you, Fred.'

He came out of the yellow public telephone booth. Francine sat waiting in the car, looking thoughtful.

'Shouldn't you tell them officially?'

'Tom was playing it close to his chest.'

'Tom's dead. Maybe that's why.'

'I'm sorry, Frankie. The way I stand with the office at the moment they'd warn me off completely. Sick leave is like suspension for me.' He started the engine. 'Anyway, I'd like to get to the bastard who caused Tom's death first.'

'Johannesburg,' she murmured.

'What?'

'The label in his hat. "Leon Bloom, Hatmaker, Johannesburg".'

Jim laughed. 'I thought for a minute you were going to say our man's name was in his hat. That went out with the initialled handkerchiefs in the old detective stories.'

He was examining the lining of the coat. It bore no label. He felt in its pockets. They had been emptied.

'Made darn sure nobody could trace him,' he said. 'I reckon any ordinary hit-and-run motorist would be in too much of a panic. He'd be shocked. This guy was used to covering his tracks.'

'But perhaps he was not quite thorough,' said Francine. She was holding up a fragment of paper. She had turned out the inner leather band of the hat and found it. All that was written on it, in biro, was V & A, 2.45.

'V & A?' Jim frowned. 'Victoria & Albert Museum.'

'Not on Jersey,' she said. 'A very discreet firm who sometimes ask the Tourism Office to make arrangements for their overseas visitors.'

'God, I am out of touch! Valentine & Angell. Arms dealers. A Johannesburg label in his hat, and an accent the girl remembered was "sort of foreign, but not".' He tried mimicking heavy South African. 'It could fit together.'

'It does,' Francine said gravely. 'Tom did Embassy duty in London – the South African Embassy.'

Jim stared at her, taking in the implications. Then he remembered one other detail.

'My ex-father-in-law's on V & A's board.'

She was surprised they were not heading back to St Helier.

'Where are we going?'

'The airport. To ask some questions. D'you mind?'

'Not at all. I like riding in your car. What is it?'

'Triumph Roadster. As the saying goes, they don't build 'em like this any more.'

Francine laughed. He was pleased to see and hear it. She may not have thought she'd be right for a copper's wife, but she seemed to have the necessary resilience.

'Jim,' she said, 'I have been thinking while you were telephoning. The medical report on you – can't you challenge it?'

'That's what I'm doing. The only way I know how. But I'd also like to finish Tom's job off for him.'

'He'd be glad to know that it might help you get yours back.'

They smiled at one another, the warm smile of already close friends.

'Will you have dinner with me?' he asked.

'Yes, I would like that.'

'The Royal Barge? I'm staying there till I find somewhere.'

'You have nowhere to live?'

'The family home's been sold up. You know what this Island's like for finding anything affordable. I'll get a service flat, I expect.'

They drove in silence for some minutes, through St John and St Mary parishes. Francine said, her eyes on the road ahead, 'My friends have lent me a place as a studio. It's a disused old building in Queen's Valley. Nothing remarkable, except it has a vineyard.'

'Working?'

'No. I think it never grew good grapes. But there is a big room downstairs. It would make a flat – if you would like it.'

'You're very kind. What would your friends say, though?'

'To be truthful, we . . . Tom and I . . . we were going to do it up, while I decided if I was right for him.'

'You take life seriously, don't you?'

'It is precious. Tom's death makes me realise it even more. My friends were intending to sell it to him. He was qualified to buy.'

'If it was good enough for Tom . . . Accepted with thanks, then.'

'You must see it first. You know where to find me.'

He drove into the airport car park. 'I won't be more than fifteen minutes. Then I'll drive you back to town.'

'Yes. I must find out what is happening to my Japanese.'

He left her in the car again and made his way to the Aero Club, where several dozen light planes stood in rows. The Chief Instructor, a laconic man of whom he had made previous police enquiries, was in the office. Omitting to tell him that he was not officially on the case, Jim said, 'I expect the Air Control people have covered all this, but I want to satisfy my own curiosity. Where do you think that plane finished up?'

'In the drink. He wasn't much of a flyer, from what I saw. He'd hardly any fuel.'

'No wreckage reported yet.'

'There will be.'

'Look, supposing he did make a landing somewhere . . .'

'No reports, either. They'll have put the word out everywhere.'

'I don't mean an airstrip. Force-landed. Crashed.'

'They'll have taken that into account.'

'Mind considering a possibility for me?'

'He flew the Atlantic? Forget it.'

Jim said, with a flash of irritation, 'One of my colleagues died trying to stop him – a pal. I want to know.'

'Sorry. What is it, then?'

'Given the weather conditions that day – cloud, windspeed, and so on – which way would he have headed?'

'Almost certainly south-west. There was a strong head wind from the East – Normandy. He wouldn't go that way, especially if he spotted his fuel was so low. He wouldn't want to waste much of it climbing, or going flat out, either.'

'So, where would fifteen minutes' worth get him?'

The instructor gave Jim a thinly appreciative smile at last. 'Good thinking.' He walked over to a wall chart of the Channel Islands and the French coast, far closer than England. He laid his transparent plastic ruler on it, south-westward from St Helier.

'Somewhere here, maybe. St Brieuc vicinity. Perhaps a little further south, towards Corlay.'

'Any other thoughts?'

'No. If I'd been flying it, and wasn't too bright a pilot, I bet that's where I'd have finished up.'

'Alive or dead?'

'At best, half of either. It's thick forest round there.'

'Mind if I use your phone?'

'Go ahead.'

The instructor wandered away. It was to Charlotte Jim spoke, and again he warned her to call him Fred. After he had asked her a further favour she told him she had already heard from Special Branch at the Yard, coming up with an identity for a red-headed South African in the arms business, recently spotted at both Heathrow and Gatwick, but troubled at neither because there was nothing current against him. His name was . . .

'What can I do for you, Sergeant?' asked Christopher Gurney. 'Are they thinking of arming the force at last?'

Jim straightened up from his scrutiny of a pair of pearl-handled revolvers, mounted on velvet backing in a showcase in the hallway of Valentine & Angell's offices, an elegant area belying the unpretentious front doorway in the narrow street below.

They hadn't met before. Jim had no recollection even of hearing Gurney's name. There was no reason why he should. So far as he knew, Valentine & Angell were a thoroughly reputable firm, and he had not wanted to put the willing Charlotte at further risk by asking her to make any more clandestine checks.

Gurney was in his thirties, tall, well set up, curly dark hair and watchful eyes, expensively dressed, old school tie and all.

Jim had introduced himself to the receptionist simply by his name and rank. Gurney did not bother to ask to see his badge.

'Beautiful workmanship,' Jim said, nodding towards the display.

'Superb. They belonged to William Cody – Buffalo Bill. His family came from Jersey, you know. The Le Caudeys.'

'No, I didn't know that. Charming name your company has, sir – for the arms game, I mean.'

'Hardly a game, Sergeant. Valentine & Angell have been a highly respectable institution since 1827.'

'I thought there wasn't much left in the sporting guns trade now.'

'We sell all kinds of arms. It's a business, like any other. Your department knows that.'

'Of course. Actually, I'm making enquiries about a man who might have been to see you a few days ago. We don't know his name yet, but he's believed to be South African, about forty years of age, red-haired . . .'

'I'm afraid nobody of that description has visited this office.' The reply came a shade too quickly for Jim's assurance.

'You'd know personally, sir?'

'I'm managing director. You know there is a strict embargo on the sale of arms to South Africa. No one with such connections, official or otherwise, would be dealt with except by myself, and I should entertain no sort of deal with him.'

'There are roundabout routes to most destinations.'

'Not by way of Valentine & Angell. May I ask why you thought this man came here?'

'Not thought, sir. Wondered. Routine checking.'

Gurney smiled with his lips, though not his eyes.

'Sorry I couldn't help, then.'

They shook hands, and Jim left.

He had already dropped Francine at her office. He had found himself watching her walk away from him, the jet black hair swinging from side to side.

Now he drove once more to the opulent house where he had become merely *persona semi-grata*, if indeed he had ever been more than that all along. His former father-in-law was

46

in one of his business suit phases of the day, bathed and immaculately groomed. He held his cigar in its black holder as he wandered with Jim across the hall.

'If you came to see Kim, she and Deborah are out,' he said. 'How d'you like my portrait, done for my sixtieth?' He waved the holder towards it, hanging near the foot of the sweeping staircase. 'Some French girl working on the island.'

It was Jim's first sight of any of Francine's work. His respect for her increased.

'Very good, Charlie. Bit heavy round the chin for you, perhaps, but she's got the eyes perfectly. Warm as lasers.'

Charlie Hungerford scowled. 'Now you're not family any more I can do without your cheap cracks. Why did you come here, anyway?'

'I am looking for a man I believe caused Tom Draycott's death. I'm sure he came to Jersey to do an arms deal.'

'What's that to do with me?'

'You're on the board of Valentine & Angell, that's what.'

'I don't serve at their counter. Go and talk to them.'

'I have. To the MD. Gurney.'

'And?'

'How straight is Gurney?'

'Christ! You come here suggesting I'd have anything to do with a crooked firm – arms, at that.'

'You knock buildings down, Charlie. Why not people?'

'Listen, *Sergeant*, that business is properly run. Anything illegal going on, me and the other directors would know.'

'There could always be the odd transaction behind your backs.'

'If you mean Gurney, he wouldn't sell a rifle-strap to the wrong sort of people.'

'That include South Africans?'

'You'd better be here officially to make a remark like that.'

Jim turned sharply to him, face to face. 'Name of Victor Kroll, middleman who specialises in under-the-counter shipments around the world. A ruthless bastard who doesn't care who he sells death to. Terrorists, despots, dictators, they're all his customers. That he's South African is by the way. He's so bloody evil his own country doesn't want to know him.'

'I've never heard of him, and if you've asked Chris Gurney, and he says he hasn't, you can take it as gospel. Don't you go linking a character like that with V & A in any of your computers or we'll have you personally. There are some very important names on the board, so watch it.'

'You too, Charlie. One of these days I may have to nail you – and if I have to, I will.'

'Get out!'

Down the road from the mansion he pulled up at a phone box and rang the Bureau again. Charlotte didn't bother with any more 'Fred' subterfuge. She said quickly, 'You were right. The Prefecture of police at St Malo just called to say somebody's spotted a plane wreck in a forest . . .'

'Ring them back,' he told her, glancing at his watch. 'Tell them I'm coming over on the next hydrofoil.'

He got to the harbourside as they were preparing to cast off. Leaving his car just where it stopped he ran and jumped aboard. There were no protests. The deck officer knew Jim Bergerac. Within minutes the craft was planing away, beyond the harbour limits.

The Piper Aztec had crashed nose first amongst dense trees, one half-shorn wing sticking upward like a toppled signpost. The first arrivals had already removed the pilot's body from the nearly intact cabin. He lay on a stretcher under a blanket. On a sheet nearby the contents of his pockets were neatly ranged, together with a briefcase.

The Gendarmerie inspector nodded in answer to Jim's request to examine the body and the objects. It was a red-headed man, all right. Kroll would serve as death's agent in no other cases, illicit or righteous.

Jim half-expected the briefcase to be packed tightly with wadded notes in half a dozen currencies. There were none, only papers. He read the papers, and they were more use to him than impersonal banknotes.

48

Chapter Eight

The vineyard building was low and long, built of granite and with a slate roof. It was down a rough lane off a minor road a little way inland from Gorey. The vineyard was blighted, as Francine had said.

The inside walls were untreated and the floor bare stone. Dried-up old casks and wine-pressing equipment stood about.

'This was where they pressed the grapes,' she said unnecessarily. The aroma still lingered faintly.

'So long as it doesn't turn me on again. You'll have to keep an eye on me.'

'I don't live here, only paint. I'm afraid a lot needs doing.'

'Where's your studio?'

'Upstairs.'

She led the way up a flight of wooden stairs into another room, made less gloomy than the one below by a window and skylight. The colours on canvases stacked round the walls brightened it further. One, half-finished, was on the easel. Jim was startled to recognise the sketched-in features as Christopher Gurney's.

'Do people come here to sit for you?' he asked.

'No. I go to them. Mostly in their homes. I do the finishing here.'

'Did you go to this chap's?'

'Mr Gurney? Yes, at Rozel.'

'Know much about him?'

'Not really. As a matter of fact it was your . . . Mr Hungerford who recommended me to him, after I'd done his portrait. They're on a board together.'

'That they are. V & A's.'

She stared at him.

'He didn't mention it?'

'No. He only gave me one sitting. He didn't talk about his business at all.'

'What did he talk about?'

'Oh, he breeds exotic butterflies. He was in the British Army – an officer.'

'Well-heeled? Rich?'

'I think so. In the swimming pool class. He has an expensive-looking girl friend. You remember when we were at Sorel Point, before we found the coat and hat? She waved to me from her car.'

'The coloured girl? And there was I thinking she meant it for me.'

Francine smiled. 'I should like to paint her. He has a taste for the exotic, evidently.'

'Maybe he'll commission you to do a portrait of her when you've finished him.'

'Maybe. She sings in cabarets. Her name is Juniper Green. American.' She frowned suddenly. 'But I read in the paper that she was from South Africa originally. It's a coincidence, isn't it? That man was driving towards Rozel when he knocked down that au pair girl. You don't think he was on his way to see Juniper? No, why should he?'

'I don't think he was,' Jim answered her rhetorical question. 'But I am.'

It was early evening. He guessed that Juniper Green would not be likely to leave for work until nine or so, and would probably be relaxing at the house. He didn't wish to run into Gurney, but decided to gamble that the managing director of an import company would be in the habit of spending some time at day's end in one of the clubs where top executives conducted out-of-office dealings over their gins.

He left his car in the road near the house at Rozel which Francine had described and walked tentatively up the driveway, keeping out of sight. He noticed only the American convertible they had seen Juniper driving parked in front of the house. Then he saw the girl herself, wearing a bright robe, clearing the outdoor swimming pool of leaves with a long-handled electric vacuum.

He took a chance on it and went round the house to her, introducing himself by name and rank. She flashed a mouthful of large gleaming teeth at him.

'I'm just a guest here, Sergeant. If you want Mr Gurney, he's in town.'

'That's all right. You might be able to help. You see, a few days ago a young au pair girl was knocked down on the road, just up the hill from here.'

'I never heard about any accident. But then, I don't talk much to people around here. Or rather, they don't talk much to me. Was the kid hurt bad?'

'Badly enough. The car just drove off.'

'Hit-and-run, huh? That stinks.' She switched off the vacuum. 'Wait a minute – you aren't suggesting it was me or Christopher? Because if you are, my car's right there in the driveway, and you can look it over with your magnifying glass, Sherlock. As for Christopher's Lamborghini, if there was one mark on it he'd have a nervous breakdown.'

'More caring about cars than people, is he?'

The big smile had left her face. 'What's that? Another snide crack about the arms trade? It's a respectable firm with high standards.'

'As everybody's at great pains to point out.'

'Look Sergeant, what exactly do you want?'

'I think the driver of that hit-and-run car might've been coming here.'

She turned away to put the vacuum on the ground, so that her back was to him as she answered, 'There've been no visitors lately. It's been so dull.'

'Are you sure? Aren't you out a lot, performing or rehearsing?'

'Sure. But I'm just getting over a bout of laryngitis. Lasted a fortnight. Most of the time I've stayed right here.'

She turned to face him again. He thought he had better make his throw before Gurney arrived back suddenly.

'Miss Green, you're from South Africa?'

'You been checking on me?'

'No. It was in one of your write-ups.'

'Well, that's right. I started in the clubs there when I was a kid. A scout spotted me and took me to the States. I married a Yank, but it soon bust. I couldn't take what happened in the race riots, so I quit the place and came to London. I got a season of dates over here, and Chris saw me and took me up. They didn't print that bit, though'.

'No. But it makes me even more sure you'll be interested to know that that hit-and-run driver was a white South African named Kroll. He was in the arms game, Miss Green, and not the sporting gun side of it, either. He was a supplier of weapons to any bidder. Men like that will buy from anyone who'll accept their money. In this case it was diamonds.'

He had watched her carefully as he spoke; had noticed her eyes widen slightly and flash under the impact of the revelations. He went on without pausing.

'He brought diamonds to your boy friend to pay for an illegal shipment of arms. Not from here, of course. They're in a warehouse in Denmark. Your friend wouldn't need to soil his hands with them, and he'd hardly be likely to tell you about them, in view of where they were going.'

He stopped to let her work out the implication, then asked quietly, 'Did he come here?'

She hesitated for some moments, then said, 'You're not making all this up?'

Jim shook his head. 'He got away from the Island by stealing a light aircraft. A police vehicle crashed, trying to stop him, and the driver was killed.'

She nodded. 'I heard about it on the TV.'

'That officer was my best friend. That's just part of the death and destruction that's down to Victor Kroll. He got his share of it when the plane crashed in France and he was killed. I've seen his body and read the papers in his briefcase. I know he traded diamonds with Gurney for arms for South Africa. *Did* he come here, Miss Green?'

She said numbly, 'I didn't meet him. I knew there was a visitor, but I figured it was somebody Christopher didn't

52

want to know he was keeping a girl here. A black girl. A black South African girl, in this case. Oh, that really figures!

'Did you see him at all?'

'I took a peek. Red hair?'

'That was Kroll.'

'Christopher asked if I'd seen him. I said I hadn't. When we heard about that airplane business he told me it was the same guy, but if anyone mentioned him I knew nothing.'

'Well, now you know it all. I get the impression you don't like it.'

'Are you going to pull Christopher in?'

'What do you think?'

He saw she had come to a decision. 'Wait here.' She turned towards the house.

'You're not going to use the telephone, I hope,' Jim said.

She shook her head and went quickly in. After about a minute he heard a car swish into the drive and stop. The trees whose leaves she had been clearing out of the badly sited pool offered him enough concealment. He stepped behind them.

Juniper came out again, looking round for him. She had put on a pair of skin-tight trousers and a jacket. She carried something in one hand.

He heard Gurney call her and saw him come out on to the terrace beside the pool.

'Hi!' Gurney called, grinning. 'No welcoming drink?'

She turned to him and held up her hand. Jim could see that what it held was a small bag. Gurney stared at it.

'How the hell did you get that?'

'I've known the safe combination for weeks. My insurance in case you decided to throw me out. I didn't figure on diamonds, though.'

Gurney grinned again, but uncertainly.

'Hey, who's talking about throwing you out? You shouldn't play around with those stones. They're worth a lot.'

'I bet they are.'

'A good investment just now. I got them through a broker. I was taking them to the bank tomorrow.'

'I know how you got them, Christopher, and what for. I know who your "broker" was. Only, he's dead, and he won't be collecting what he paid you these for. You never said Kroll was a white South African. You never damn well said!'

Jim saw from Gurney's changed look that he was calculating some move. He might be planning merely to snatch the bag of diamonds, but he would not put it beyond him to topple Juniper backwards into the pool and make sure she drowned. He was starting to edge towards her.

'It had nothing to do with you,' he was saying.

'Nothing? Look at the colour of my skin!'

'You know we deal with all sorts of people and countries. This was just a deal. No politics involved.'

'But you knew where those arms would go. You damn well knew!'

He lunged towards her. Simultaneously, as Jim leaped from cover, Juniper swung round and held the bag upside down over the pool. The diamonds scattered into it like water droplets.

Her action halted Gurney, who stared into the pool. 'You stupid bitch!' he shouted, and turned to her again, but saw Jim coming towards them. With a sudden movement Gurney grabbed the pool-vacuum from the ground and swung it. It hit Jim on the thigh of his injured leg, hurting him like hell. He paid no regard to regulations about the use of minimal force in making an arrest. After a brief wrestle Gurney finished up in the pool, along with his diamonds.

'Thanks,' Jim said to Juniper. 'Go and call the police, will you? Say you're speaking for Jim Bergerac. It'll bring them, if only from curiosity.'

She went in, leaving him to stand watch over the floundering figure, holding the vacuum pipe with which both of them knew he wouldn't hesitate to belt him if he tried to climb out.

Like most good policemen, Jim never looked for the reward of personal publicity in connection with his successful results. This time, when he saw that the *Jersey Evening Post* had mentioned his name prominently and added a paragraph about his having made the enquiries leading to this arrest while on sick leave following serious injury, he grinned.

The Chief did not grin when he read it, and was not surprised to receive an early visit from the Senator who presided over the Police Committee. They held some earnest conversation before summoning Jim in.

'What the hell were you playing at?' the Chief demanded when the full story had been recited. 'Keeping Crozier right out of the picture. Going off to Brittany to look at a crashed aircraft we'd not even heard about . . .'

'Recuperating, sir. Sick leave.'

'Only one thing to be done,' said the silver-haired Senator, maintaining a straight face. 'If he can do that on sick leave, he might as well be on duty while he waits for his board.'

'I believe there is a desk free, somewhere in the Bureau,' the Chief nodded. 'No point in wasting resources.'

'Thank you, Chief,' said Jim.

The Island had accepted him back.

Chapter Nine

The hotel was one of the Island's biggest and best, resembling a French château as it glistened white in the floodlighting. The car park in front was packed, the big public rooms on the ground floor were ablaze with lights and noise from a big band and a throng of well-heeled revellers.

Dinner jackets and evening gowns were the order in the Atlantic Suite, where the tables were ranged around an illuminated swimming pool into which someone would almost inevitably fall or be pushed before the evening was out. A tombola ticket drum and a mass of prizes occupied a table to one side, where a brash Master of Ceremonies waited, microphone at the ready, to breeze in whenever the band paused.

Out in the deeply carpeted foyer a function board on an ornate easel announced: 'Channel Islands Society Charity Fund dinner – 8 pm. Guest of Honour – Sir Edward Lister.'

The function was in full swing; had been for two hours. Sir Edward Lister had not yet made his entrance, though. He would not be doing so. Upstairs, in the hotel's best suite, he was lying down, fully clothed. Lying down dead.

Because Sir Edward Lister was a visitor from mainland Britain, the doctor's telephone call was routed to the Bureau des Étrangers. Jim Bergerac was the DS on duty. He made a note in the log and went to the hotel without inordinate haste.

The doctor was coughing his lungs up in the bathroom when Jim entered the penthouse suite. He grinned. Physician, convince thyself that forty fags a day is not good medicine.

'Still at it, Dennis,' he called.

Dr Dennis Lejeune emerged, drying his hands on a towel,

56

spluttering around the cigarette between his lips. He was a cynical man, heavily bearded, in his forties. He made a wry face, threw the towel into a chair and removed the cigarette, indicating with it the bedroom adjoining. They went through. On the large bed an elderly man lay. Apart from some distortion of the face, and the opened shirt front where Dennis Lejeune had been listening to the chest, Jim could see nothing untoward. The body might have been laid out already, it was so neatly disposed.

'Charity big-wheel,' the doctor wheezed. 'Director of the Overseas Famine Foundation.'

Jim straightened up to glance about the suite.

'They don't stint themselves, do they?' he said. 'No wonder some charities cost as much to run as they dole out.'

'Luxury isn't much use to him now,' came the laconic reply. 'Sudden cardiac arrest. Out like a light.'

'Why bring in the Bureau, then?'

'Eminent visitor, for starters.'

'Something else?'

'Unless you regard it natural for a dead man to walk.'

'Walk?'

'His wife thinks he died where he is. Just lay down and had the attack. I don't, I think he was put there.'

'Perhaps whoever found him . . .'

'She found him. He was here, like this.'

'Maybe he collapsed in the bathroom or somewhere. Dragged himself back here . . .'

'Then straightened himself out on the bed, put his hands by his sides, and expired? It's too neat, Jim. Too arranged. He'd have thrashed around.'

'The trouble with you police doctors is you wish you could swap places with us detectives.'

'The trouble with you detectives is you don't detect. Sand on his shoes, but none on the carpet or the bed. And where'd he get paint on himself in here?'

The doctor indicated a blue-green smudge on one of the trouser legs. Jim touched it and examined his finger. It was paint all right. He looked at the shoes. Damp sand had dried between the uppers and soles.

'You talked much to his wife?' he frowned.

'Briefly. She's in shock.'

'She wasn't here when it happened, then?'

'She was down at the dinner.'

'She went but he didn't?'

'He isn't dressed for it, is he? Lounge suit.'

'You get cleverer, Dennis.'

The doctor was too overcome by another coughing fit to respond. He struggled into his coat and got his bag.

'Can you manage to tell me who called you?' Jim asked.

'The hotel manager. He was told by some young clergyman on this chap's staff. Name of Cassell.'

'Where's he now — and the widow?'

'They organised another suite for her. They'll be there.'

'Meanwhile the show goes on.'

'They decided not to announce it. Just that he was indisposed. Think of all those charity funds they're busy raising. I'll do an autopsy in the morning. 'Night, Jim.'

He coughed his way out of the suite.

Lady Lister proved to be elegant, dark-haired, coldly attractive in a brocaded silk gown with a deeply plunging neckline. Allowing for the beauty specialists' attentions she would would be ten or more years younger than her late husband.

The clergyman-aide was in attendance on her, a tall, pale, but handsome young man in a dark suit and dog collar. Peter Cassell returned Jim a limp handshake.

'He'd had no warning, no previous attacks,' Lady Lister said. 'That's the cruel thing, when you just get the one and you're gone.'

'I'm sorry to have to question you at such a time,' Jim told her, 'but why wasn't your husband at the function?'

'He went out of the hotel about six. He said there was some delegate of the conference whom he needed to talk to privately.'

'He was guest of honour, though. Any idea who this other person was, or why it was so important?'

Cassell intervened. 'We've no idea at all. We'd all packed

up after the day's session. Sir Edward was looking forward to the dinner.'

'Yet he didn't come back in time.'

Lady Lister explained, 'I telephoned the suite twice from downstairs, in case he'd come in, but there was no answer. I left the dinner before the speeches and came up. I . . . I can hardly bear to tell you this, Sergeant, but I never thought to go into the bedroom. I just sat down in the lounge and kicked my shoes off and watched television. A programme about Tahiti. Can you imagine it – I was watching hula dancers with my husband lying through there . . . If I'd gone in sooner I might have saved him.'

She was sobbing. Cassell, standing beside her, placed a hand on her shoulder.

'I don't think you could have done anything,' Jim reassured her, and left them.

On his way out of the hotel he asked the doorman, an old acquaintance, to point out Sir Edward Lister's car. Then he went and examined its tyres and wheels. It had been driven on sand.

Dr Lejeune was lighting up a cigarette after washing his hands and arms. The mortuary attendant was wheeling away the stretcher trolley on which the body lay covered. The door was held open for him by Barney Crozier, who happened to be coming in.

'What the hell goes on?' the Inspector demanded. 'Why wasn't I told? A report should have been on my desk first thing.'

Jim glanced at his watch. 'It's only ten minutes past first thing, Barney.'

He got a scowl in return. 'All I get is a bloody message summoning me to the Presence. What's it about?'

'Just that Sir Edward didn't die on his bed, where he was found.'

'It could have been someone else's bed, though,' the doctor amplified. 'In it.'

Crozier stared at him. 'How d'you make that out?'

'Because he was dressed after death. Lower shirt-button in the wrong buttonhole. The way his tie knot was done up. Sand in his shoes.'

'So, he'd got dressed in a hurry and walked on a beach. It happens.'

'Sand *in* his shoes, Barney,' Jim corrected him. 'As well as on them. You usually shake them out, don't you?'

'Well . . . anything else?'

Dr Lejeune said, 'It's possible he was in a scuffle. There's a slight knuckle bruise, consistent with throwing a punch. Also some bruising on the chest, though that could've resulted from attempts to revive him. My advice, *mes amis*, is *cherchez la femme*.'

He picked up a jacket which Jim recognised as the one the dead man had been wearing and thrust it towards each of them to sniff at. There was a distinct odour of Rive Gauche on it.

'Oh God!' Crozier groaned. 'He was with another woman. That'll fetch the mainland Press. Pillar of respectability and all that. Sexual exertion, was it?'

'No signs. Can't have got that far.'

'That's something, then. Maybe they had a row – triggered off his heart attack. She panicked, dressed him somehow, lugged him back to the hotel . . .'

'She'd have needed to be built like a Russian discus thrower to manage him.'

'She got help.'

The doctor threw his cigarette end into a white pail, where it was extinguished with a hiss.

'Take two to carry him, for sure,' he confirmed. 'And hardly through the foyer.'

'Watch this chap,' Jim warned his superior, as he made for the door. 'He fancies himself for next Chief.'

'More chance than you,' came the sour response. 'Where are you going?'

'I want to talk to his assistant again, before I tackle Lady L.'

'Remember, then – keep me informed.'

'Yes, *Inspector*.'

Jersey's latest and most lavish man-made centre of tourist attraction is the Fort Regent complex. Where British soldiers in red coats once drilled in anticipation of Napoleonic onslaught which did not come, and Germans, who did come, kept stores and manned guns which never needed to be fired in anger, the less grim pursuits of dancing, drinking, eating, swimming, bowling, roller skating, squash, giant chess, watching top showbiz acts, and a host of other sports and pastimes are now enjoyed in five million pounds' worth of development of the massive old fortress, towering high over St Helier.

There are also less frivolous activities: classical concerts, exhibitions, trade fairs; and such earnest excuses for a few days' expenses-paid swanning as enjoyed by the delegates to the eighth International Charities Co-ordinating Conference.

In high season, those who do not suffer too severely from vertigo can travel up to the Fort by closed cable car. Those who prefer not to swing through the air can drive or use the long, glass-sided escalator, which offers the same panoramic view plus a greater feeling of stability.

Jim travelled up by the escalator for the renewed experience. It was his first trip up there since returning to the Island, but he paid no attention to the view. His eyes were for Francine, who had spotted him and lingered behind some other uniformed Tourism Office girls.

'"Francine Leland",' he read aloud from the badge on her lapel. '*Excusez-moi, m'selle* – about the accommodation you found me . . .'

'Jim!' She looked up from her clipboard. 'Where have you been lately?'

'More at the vineyard than you.'

'I've been run off my feet with this charity thing. They keep changing their plans. How's the decorating going?'

'Could be more progress with your aid and inspiration.'

'I'm sorry. As soon as I can. What are you doing here? Coming to view "the fabulous Jersey Experience, using the latest audio/visual techniques to create in sound and vision the Story of Jersey"?'

'Seen it so often with Kim I could recite it for them if the equipment breaks down. No, I want to talk to one of the British delegates to the conference. A young clergyman named Cassell.'

'Ah yes, I know. He is ... was assistant to Sir Edward Lister. They are all very shaken about him dying suddenly. You heard?'

'I heard.'

'Today's session has been delayed till after lunch, out of respect.'

'How do you show respect for a man's charity work by knocking off for the morning and doing the shops?'

'Ah, you are a cynic. But he was such a nice man, Sir Edward.'

'You met him?'

'I met them at the airport. I thought his wife rather cold but he was *charmant*.'

'You find older men attractive?'

'We French girls often do.'

'I'll remember that. D'you think he fancied you?'

'He behaved like a perfect English gentleman.' She frowned slightly, because his question had sounded not altogether flippant. 'Why do you ask?'

'Perhaps I'll tell you some day.'

They came off the escalator. Francine hurried on to rejoin her colleagues and Jim made for the massive Conference Centre. Attendants were re-erecting rows of stowaway chairs. He recognised Cassell looking on, now dressed in casual clothes. Jim was surprised. He expected him to be in full clerical rig, so soon after his master's death.

'Mr Cassell,' he greeted him, 'I need your help.'

'Ah. About the arrangements?'

'Arrangements?'

'For flying Sir Edward's body home. Lady Lister's staying with the Senator until ...'

'No, not that. Not strictly my province – but I think it will have to wait a day or two yet. Clearance takes a little longer in Jersey.'

'You make it sound like Customs.'

'Sorry. It's your help I need. It's a bit . . . delicate. Free for a coffee?'

At a table in a concourse café he stirred his coffee and went on.

'I have to ask this, Mr Cassell. Next to his wife, you'd be closest to him most of the time?'

It was merely a discreet opening, but it got a sharp glance.

'Would you know if he was playing around? Having an affair?'

Cassell regarded him with something like distaste.

'Are all you Channel Islanders quite so direct?'

'*Was* he, Mr Cassell?'

'He . . . was a socialiser. It was part of his job.'

'Socialising with any lady in particular, while you've been here?'

'Look, Sergeant, I can understand the newspaper people trying to dig up dirt to discredit charity organisers for a story. But why you?'

'We think Sir Edward might have been with another woman when he died.'

'That is a most offensive suggestion!'

'Is that a personal reaction or an official one? For the charity? For his wife?'

Cassell had flushed deeply. 'I was his assistant, not his keeper. If there had been . . . anything, I wouldn't regard it as my concern.'

'You wouldn't go out of your way to cover anything up, then?'

'It doesn't arise. He had a heart attack and he died. Isn't that enough?' He got up. 'Thanks for the coffee. I've got things to supervise in there.'

He went off. Jim got up to pay the bill. He had hoped to get to it more easily, without hurting Lady Lister with what might yet prove only to be a supposition. But it was going to have to be the hard way.

She received him on the terrace outside the Senator's fine white house, sitting looking down on the beach and a poun-

63

ding sea. The sunshine seemed to have thawed her a little. But she said, 'I feel numb. Sort of disassociated. As though everything's suddenly halted.'

'You had a busy life together?'

'Always travelling. Jet-lag, sleeping pills, official functions, dinners. Ironic, isn't it, banquets in aid of the starving? But how else do you get money out of the rich? Maybe that was it – like ocean cruises, when people pay so much they want to eat their money's worth. And then Nature has her revenge. But why Edward? He was so good. He cared so.'

'Why, indeed?'

She turned to study him in the chair next to her. 'There's something in your eyes that tells me you mean that question. Why did you come here to see me?'

When travelling an uncertain route, the straightest way often proves the most expeditious. 'Because we don't think your husband died where you found him.'

He was watching her keenly as he said it. Her surprised response seemed genuine.

'I . . . don't understand.'

'We believe your husband wasn't in the hotel when he died. Someone brought him there afterwards.'

'You're not making sense. Please.'

'It's how it appears. Perhaps the circumstances . . .'

'What circumstances?'

'Panic. Fear. I'm sorry, Lady Lister, I have to come to this sooner or later. From certain evidence it's a fair assumption he was undressed at the time he died. His clothes were put on him.'

He knew as he was saying it that her reaction would be significant. She would jump up and order him off the premises, or shriek at him, or burst into tears, or . . .

'Bergerac!' It was the Senator calling from the open French doors. 'A telephone call for you. They say it's very urgent.'

Jim got up.

'Excuse me,' he said to Lady Lister.

She didn't reply. She was sitting perfectly still, with her head bowed.

Chapter Ten

He was at the hotel within minutes of being called to the Senator's phone. The manager and a chambermaid were waiting for him in a room at the back of the hotel, along the corridor from the suite the Listers had occupied. It was Cassell's, and it had been ransacked.

'When did this happen?' he asked.

'Within the last hour, apparently,' the manager said. 'I got them to put me on to you personally because you seemed to be dealing with these people's affairs.'

'Thanks.'

'They must have come and gone by the fire escape. The window was wide open when Doris came in to collect his coffee things.'

'That's right,' the middle-aged maid confirmed. 'Mr Cassell was in here working an hour ago when I brought the coffee. When I came back he'd gone and it was like this. I telephoned down straight away.'

Jim could see that it had been done comprehensively, but unprofessionally.

'What on earth's been going on here?' Cassell had come into the room, carrying his briefcase.

'Thanks again,' Jim said to the manager, who took the hint and went, taking the maid with him. Jim closed the door and turned to Cassell.

'Your room's been done over. What were they after?' He was direct and tough.

'I've no idea . .'

'Come on. Who are they? What's it about?'

'Well . . . all right. You see, we'd been planning to produce a sort of mild earthquake at the conference tomorrow. There's a highly confidential document. There could be

65

someone interested in stopping us.'

'Who's "us"?'

'Sir Edward, originally. After his death I consulted Lady Lister and she agreed he'd have wanted me to carry on.'

'What's it about?'

'For over a year we've suspected that large sums of charity money have been misused by a Central American regime. Last time we visited the place some students gave us a secret memorandum they'd somehow got hold of. It was written by one of their senior finance officials. It makes it quite plain how the money's being spent – and it isn't on public welfare, believe me.'

'Who knew about this besides you and the Listers?'

'Quite a few people. Sir Edward was lining up support for a crucial vote to stop funds going there.'

'So it could be any of dozens, maybe, who might have leaked this to others. Well, I suppose you've had it now, if they've pinched your memo.'

For once Cassell smiled. He patted his briefcase.

'They haven't. It's in here.'

Jim relaxed and grinned. 'Good for you, then. In that case, it's OK to let them come and clean up this mess for you.'

'Do we need to tell Diana . . . Lady Lister?'

'That's your decision,' said Jim; and wondered. 'I'd keep your window locked until you've pulled off your coup, though.'

'I will.'

They were at the door. Jim nodded and went out. He was just turning to go, and the door was closing on him, when out of the corner of his eye he caught a blur of movement in the room. He heard Cassell shout. He shoved the door and ran back in. The door of the big walk-in wardrobe was wide open and a figure in jeans and bomber jacket was leaving fast by the floor-length window.

Jim barged across the room, cursing himself for having taken it for granted that the intruder had already gone.

Feet clattered on the iron fire escape. He saw, a flight below, a dark-haired young man, a glimpse of beard and the glint of metal spectacle frames as he swung round one of the landings of the green-painted stairs.

66

'Hold it there!' Jim yelled, hoping at least for an upward glance of the full face. There was none. He started off down the stairs, realising at once that, as sound as he believed his leg to be, a steep downward chase like this was one test those hospital sadists hadn't thought of.

The pain was fierce, but he was doing well. His quarry realised his closeness. He paused to drag a chubby red fire extinguisher off its bracket, swung round, and flung it at Jim. It was strongly thrown and well aimed, bouncing off the rail to strike his injured leg, luckily not squarely but causing him to lose his footing. The mechanism was triggered by impact. Foam engulfed him. He struggled to hold on, slipped, slid, and toppled down the stairs.

In those seconds, his dread was that his leg was going to smash again. That would be the end. It might as well be his neck. There was a smudge of white, as a car squealed forward below. The man he had pursued flung himself into it and it roared away. Clinging to the rail, where he had finished up, Jim was just able to focus his eyes and wits on the rear numberplate with its letter H, signifying a hire car.

Then feet were clattering down above him, and Cassell's voice asking if he was all right. As he let himself be helped up, gingerly testing his limbs one by one, he believed he could say he was – except that his trousers were soaked with fire extinguisher foam, and his hands were sticky and blue-green from the recently painted metal staircase.

He let Cassell assist him round to the front of the hotel and into the foyer, where people stared at the sight. He used the reception desk telephone to call the Bureau.

'Charlotte – get out an alert, fast. White Ford Escort . . .' He told her the hire firm and the approximate registration number. 'Harbour and airport. I'll explain later to our mutual friend, your boss. Who? Dr Lejeune? OK, I'll go right to him, then I'm coming in.'

He took a taxi from the hotel to the mortuary, probing his leg on the way, feeling thankful he wasn't being driven there in a different capacity. Dennis Lejeune, whose sense of humour was as morbid as many another forensic doctor's,

67

made him lie on the autopsy table to be examined.

'You're all right,' he said at length. 'Messy, but intact.'

Jim swung himself stiffly down.

'Thanks. Charlotte said you'd called me.'

'Right. Something I found I'd overlooked about Lister. He wasn't wearing his watch.'

'Are you sure he ever did?'

'Almost permanent indentation above the wrist. Hairs worn off. Metal strap, I'd say.'

'Thanks. Told the Bureau?'

'It's your case, isn't it, Jim?'

'Thanks again.'

He telephoned from there to the Senator's house and spoke to Lady Lister. She sounded annoyed.

'The Senator took me to see Inspector Crozier. He said you had no instructions to come questioning me. I made it plain that I simply wish to be left alone until I leave for home.'

'I'm sorry, Lady Lister. It's a small point, but it could be important. Your late husband's watch . . .'

'Yes?'

'What sort was it?'

'I don't see what . . .'

'It wasn't on him. What sort was it, please?'

'Well . . . gold. I don't know what make. He was a Member of Parliament in the 'sixties. His constituency presented him with it.'

'Inscribed?'

'Yes.'

'Thank you. I apologise for troubling you and I'll try not to again.'

'Do that, please.' She hung up.

He reached the Bureau just as Crozier was leaving the building in a hurry.

'What the hell have you been up to now?' the Inspector asked, staring at his sodden and paint-stained clothes.

'Painting my digs. Sloppy worker.'

'Like hell! I've got things to say to you, but I've got to get over to Guernsey fast. I'll want you when I get back.'

'*Bien sûr*, Barney.'

The Inspector curled his lip and dashed into his waiting car, to be whisked away. Jim went on up to the Bureau. Charlotte took one look at him and whistled.

'One crack about what I've done to myself . . .' he warned her.

'I wasn't going to say a word. You've just missed Mr Crozier.'

'Near-miss, in fact.'

'And the airport called a second ago. Your white hire car's been picked up and a man and a woman held.'

'Thanks, love. Tell 'em I'll be right there. And put a gold wrist watch on the stolen list – inscribed to Sir Edward Lister.'

'Who's a busy boy, then?'

He leaned over and gave her a kiss on her dimpled cheek. Then he hurried out and down again, to get a car to the airport.

'Who do they say they are?' he asked the plainclothes constable beside him. He was in the airport police office, peering through a slat of venetian blind at the couple who lounged morosely in the interview room, watched over by a uniformed security man.

'Josie Rush and George Morell. She's a journalist, he's a photographer. Some fringe rag in London. Don't they look it?'

'Never tell these days. Could be *The Times*.'

The bearded Morell had his booted feet up on a bench. His jeans were heavily stained with the blue-green paint. The girl, pretty but scruffy, was lighting a cigarette. The table was strewn with a tape machine, camera and camera case and other pieces of equipment.

'Quite a scuffle when we grabbed them,' the constable said. 'If she is a writer, her vocabulary's all four-letter words. You might learn some new ones.'

He didn't, but he gleaned a good deal more, though it was given reluctantly, following the usual tedious harangue about the freedom of the Press and the tyranny of editors over staff who didn't get their stories.

'Where does assaulting a police officer come in?' Jim said.
'Look,' the girl insisted, 'he didn't know you were a cop.'
'Breaking and entering, then?'
'Journalists sometimes have to work that way.'
'You're down on the police quick enough if we step an inch out of line.'
'There's a different set of rules for pigs,' said Morell.

Jim reached out and flipped the man's feet off the bench. He stood over him.

'You call me "pig" just once more, Morell, and I'll stand on your cameras, your hands, and then your head. And I'll smile while I'm doing it.'

It was as well for Morell, if he had intended retorting, that the door opened just then and the CID man looked in. 'Jim,' he beckoned. Jim gave Morell a glare and went into the corridor.

'You put out a check for a missing watch?' the constable asked.

'Yes.'

'Bloke tried to sell it half an hour ago. The jeweller turned it down. He only got notification after the chap had gone.'

'Damn!'

'It's all right. He knows him. Name of Mandara. Nino Mandara, waiter at the Paradise Beach Hotel. Italian.'

'I'm on my way. Leave these two muck-rakers to cook awhile. Put 'em in separate rooms, so they can't use what minimal journalistic skills they may have to work out some plausible story.'

'Won't he still be going the rounds with the watch – other jewellers?'

'I doubt it. That turn-down will have scared him. He'll try flogging it to some tourist in a bar tonight.'

He drove at once to the ungraded motel-type establishment behind one of the Island's least attractive beaches. It looked deserted now. The only person in the reception area was a slight young man with Latin good looks of the non-classical variety. He was dressed in jeans and a denim shirt and was reading a newspaper at the desk.

'You Nino?' asked Jim. He sensed at once that the man had picked him for a copper.

'*Si*, Nino Mandara.'

'I hear you've a watch for sale.'

Jim's hand snaked out and grabbed Nino's wrist. The watch on it was a cheap one, but the breast pocket of the shirt sagged under the weight of the one he was after. He drew it out.

'Police,' said Jim. 'Sergeant Bergerac. Talk.'

Nino licked his lips. 'I found it, *signore*.'

'Or took it off him.'

'Off who?'

'The man who died. Sir Edward Lister.'

'I know nothing of him.'

'There's his name on it – see.'

'Honest, *signore*, I know nothing of this man.'

'Where did you find it, then?'

'It was this morning. When I go to take the linen. It was on the floor, almost under the bed. I have no way of tracing them, so I keep it to take to the police when I am in St Helier next.'

'You tried to flog it there already. The owner of this watch is dead, Nino. We're not very happy about the circumstances. You have his watch. You're in trouble, son.'

The Italian's face had gone very white. He said quickly, 'Sergeant, I swear to you I know nothing. The manager is away and I am in charge. A girl came and offered me thirty pounds to let a chalet for one night.'

'Thirty pounds in this dump! Too much to hope she signed the register?'

'It was a private deal. *Signore*, if you will please not tell the boss when he comes.'

'I doubt you'll be here then. What else did the deal involve?'

'I have to keep out of sight and mind my business. There is no guests now. I stay in the bar with some vino and do as she has said.'

'Who was she, this girl?'

'She never tell me her name.'

Jim described the arrested journalist. Nino scratched his head in a show of uncertainty, but it was not well done.

'Hot-blooded Italian like you would have noticed,' Jim said. 'Who else came?'

'I tell you, I don't look. There was a car, maybe two, drive to the chalet and later away, but nothing more.'

'What time was this?'

'I don't notice. Nine, ten.'

'You'll need to remember sooner or later. Meantime, show me.'

The man took a key from a peg and led the way to the chalets, occupying an area of neglected sandy ground. Jim thought that if this place ever sought a grading it would need a lot doing to it. The room was furnished with the minimum essentials for one-night occupants: bed, chest of drawers, washbasin. A white duvet and a blanket were folded on the bed, but there was no linen.

'No maid service?' Jim observed.

Nino shrugged. 'Just me now. I take the linen away. Someone else is coming, I give them another chalet. Is saving work.'

'So is not emptying the wastepaper bin, I see.' Jim picked up the tin receptacle and tipped its contents on to the bed. He found three cigarette ends, all stained with lipstick, a lipstick-marked tissue, and an empty perfume spray. He used the clean part of the tissue to pick up the spray and sniff it. Then he wrapped it and the butts in the tissue.

'You say you never came in here till this morning? Didn't hang around like a peeping-Tom?'

'What is that, *signore*?'

'Listening. Taking a look.'

'I swear, sir. I hear nothing, I see nothing. I am happy with thirty pounds.'

'When's your boss due back?'

'Tonight. Sir, you will please say nothing . . .?'

'He may get to read it in the newspaper, depending how much I find you're really involved. Come on. I'm not taking you in, but I want your passport.'

72

'Well?' he said to Josie Rush half an hour later. 'Thought any useful thoughts while I've been away?'

She was alone in the airport interview room, guarded by a security man outside the door. She returned him a sullen stare and stubbed out her cigarette. The packet lay beside the ashtray. Jim took it, drew out a cigarette and inspected it.

'You going to take my ciggies away now?' she said contemptuously.

He returned it to the pack and pushed it back across the table to her. 'Handbag,' he ordered. She seemed about to refuse so he reached out and took it. He rummaged amongst its contents.

'No lipstick?'

'I don't use any.'

'Perfume?'

'I've run out.'

'And you didn't buy any more here, where it's cheap?'

'We *were* in rather a hurry.'

'I bet.' He brought from his pocket the empty container in the tissue and showed it her. 'This yours?'

She shook her head. 'I wouldn't use that stuff.'

He lifted her open handbag and sniffed inside. Then he put the empty spray to his nose. The smells didn't match.

'Told you,' she said.

'All right,' Jim said, shoving the handbag back to her, 'let's stop messing around. You've already admitted you were after that report Sir Edward Lister was going to make public. I suppose one of his loyal associates tipped your paper off about it and you were sent to get the story before anyone else.'

'You know we don't reveal our sources.'

'It's your methods that interest me. The hotel tell me you tried to get an interview with Lister the day before but you were turfed out.'

'The bloody manager wouldn't even let them ring his room to ask. I'm an accredited journalist.'

'And a woman. You already knew what I've come to suspect – that Lister was a compulsive womaniser. You got

73

to him somehow, took him to that beach hotel and got him into bed, while your photographer friend waited for you to get busy and then take a compromising picture. That way, you were sure he'd hand over the memo to keep you quiet.'

'You've got a filthy mind!' She was flushing deeply.

He ignored it. 'It went wrong, didn't it? When Morell came in with his camera and Lister saw how he'd been tricked he started raving. Then the totally unpredicted happened. He had a heart attack. Pegged out on you. That really scared you both. You put his clothes on him, drove him back to the hotel, and lugged him up the fire escape to his room. If you'd chucked him on the floor you might just have got away with it, instead of laying him out on his bed.'

The girl was staring at him with an expression blending disbelief, fright, and utter contempt. She stood up and said with acid bitterness, 'And they say it's always journalists who twist things. I've never gone in for cop-bashing in my stories but now I see why it happens.'

Still seated, Jim produced the gold watch and held it up by its band. 'Lister's. Found in the chalet. The one thing you didn't put back on him.'

The effect on her was not the dramatic one he had anticipated. She sat down again, slowly, and said in a quiet voice, 'There's something you'd better know.'

'Good,' he went on, experiencing that satisfaction which comes when a suspect realises it is hopeless to go on and tells all.

She was shaking her head.

'I write as Josie Rush. It's my maiden name. My married name's Morell. You've got my husband next door. If you want to go in there and suggest that he let his wife make a whore of herself just to get a story, you'd better not go alone.'

Chapter Eleven

If he had been a drinking man still he would have headed for the airport bar to wash the foul taste off his tongue. He knew she had told him the truth, and that he had insulted her vilely.

Because he despised journalists who cared nothing for laws or personal privacy; because he disliked arrogance and scruffiness; because, most of all, the man had called him 'pig': for these reasons, and his impatience to show Barney Crozier who was the better copper, he had let himself be blindly misled by circumstantial evidence.

It wasn't beyond belief that husband and wife journalists might degrade themselves in pursuit of a story. But he was sure these two hadn't. He looked beyond their scruffy style, their insulting sarcasm, and reminded himself that even nowadays, when morality is valued pretty cheaply, everyone save psychopaths and the worst of villains and yobs has a personal line drawn somewhere.

Jim Bergerac belonged to the Island, where many of the old values still prevailed. He had grown up with them. It was why he had married Deborah – mistake though it had turned out to be: he had conceived it his duty, and would have felt himself cheap not to have done it. If he was above cheapening himself, why shouldn't he believe it of these two?

Policemen do not apologise readily, but again his self-respect insisted that he should. The girl obviously recognised what made him do so, and thanked him, volunteering to make a statement with her husband about the unauthorised entry to Cassell's room. He told her it wouldn't be necessary and that he didn't propose to charge Morell with assaulting him. He merely took their address and told her they could go.

'Do you think there is a story in Lister's death?' she asked, journalistic instinct prevailing still.

'No. Forget it.'

'But all this about . . .'

'Mrs Morell, you were leaving the Island when you were detained. Just carry on, eh?'

She even gave him a smile. 'All right.'

'And we don't like being called pigs – though I'm fond of the creatures myself.'

'Point taken.'

They shook hands. He called the constable to take her to her husband and make sure they got a flight. Then he left the airport and drove to the vineyard, to carry on with some therapeutic decorating while he tried to reassemble his thoughts into some different pattern.

Before taking off his jacket he took from its pocket the tissue and placed it and the empty perfume container on the coffee table, one of the unremarkable pieces of furniture he had bought, and dropped the cigarette ends into the ashtray on it. He had a couch, a few chairs, a small mule chest, some loose rugs, his hi-fi equipment. It had needed remarkably little work to transform the disused room into an embryo of the sort of setting which gets photographed for the glossy house and home journals.

Utility having had to come before decoration, he was painting his way round the walls, one by one, all in white to lighten the low room.

'Ah!' exclaimed Francine, walking in. '*Bien amusant.*'

'Hello. Well, what d'you think?'

'Remarkable. Just a little more work and it will be *très chic.*'

'No thanks. Come to help?'

'If you wish it . . .' She broke off. He saw that she was looking at the coffee table. ' . . . Though if you have company . . .'

'Company?' He was amused to see her regarding the litter on the table top. 'Oh, the other woman, you mean. She's hiding behind the sofa.'

He put down the paint roller and went to her side.

'No, in fact I brought those bits from the Paradise Beach Hotel. It's possible Sir Edward Lister was there with a woman.'

'That place?'

'Less conspicuous than most.'

'But you're not serious?'

'I thought I was. I'm beginning to wonder.'

He told her briefly of the collapse of his seemingly certain case against the journalists, and how badly he felt at having misjudged them so readily.

'It must have seemed obvious,' she commented, sounding rather touched by his confession. 'But, Jim, it's as well you are painting this place only white.'

'Eh?'

'You have not much eye for colour, it seems.'

'Come on, Frankie. What is it?'

She pointed to the cigarette stubs. 'Two different shades of lipstick. Two women. Perhaps it's not surprising he had a heart attack.'

He was peering at them, acknowledging how right she was, when the telephone began to ring upstairs. It was an amenity Francine needed for her job, and Jim had been glad to find it installed. He had given the number to a few people who might want him urgently.

It was for him. Charlotte, at the Bureau. 'Jim, someone called Roger wants you to go over quickly. Rather, his sister was calling for him. Said you'd understand.'

'Thanks, love. Barney back yet?'

'Not yet. Had to stop over. Mr Cassell's called twice for him. Says Lady Lister's getting impatient to leave the island.'

'She'll have to wait. No developments?'

'I was going to ask you'

'I'll keep in touch.'

'I've got to pop out,' he told Francine. 'An AA call.'

'AA?'

'Alcoholics Anonymous. We each have certain contacts we ring if we need help. That was a message from one of mine.'

'Ah, well . . . Shall I carry on for you?'

'If you think plain white emulsion paint isn't beneath you.'

She smiled. Their friendship had progressed to the stage where little jibes at one another were in order, as harmless as puppies' sparring with clawless paws, and as affectionate.

He drove to the small house on the edge of St Helier where Roger lived with his sister. Roger was ten years older than Jim and had been drinking correspondingly longer. It showed in his fat, lumpy face. He was a worrier. The more he worried, the more he drank, and worried about it, in a vicious circle. His greatest fear, underlying it all, was that as a self-employed taxi driver he was sooner or later going to find himself banned or smashed up.

Alcoholics Anonymous, to which Jim had been recommended by the remedial therapists, had helped Roger get it under control, too, but he was liable to break out every now and then. Jim knew this call for help signified one of those lapses. He had become Roger's special counsellor in the organisation.

The overweight figure was slouched at the table of the kitchen he also used as an office. He was looking thoroughly sorry for himself. His older sister appeared no happier.

'She made me call you,' he apologised to Jim. 'I'd only had two.'

'Two-thirds,' she corrected. 'Two-thirds of the bottle.'

'I feel bloody awful,' Roger moaned.

'Fatal to his job, I keep telling him. I poured the rest of it down the sink. I'm not standing here and watch you ruin yourself, I said.'

'You got any more stashed away, Roger?'

'No.'

'He bloody well has. Haven't you?'

'Leave me alone, can't you?'

'Come on,' said Jim, taking his arm. 'Let's have a look.'

Instinct told him where it would be, and it was; under the back seat of the taxicab. It was wrapped in a rag, a full half-bottle of whisky.

Jim handed it to Roger.

'Throw it away,' he ordered.

Roger hesitated, looking at the bottle.

'If he won't, I will,' his sister said.

'No. He must. Do it, Roger.'

Roger drew back his arm and hurled the bottle from him. It shattered on a rockery, giving the straggly plants an alcoholic soaking.

He turned away. 'Good of you to come, Jim. You know how it is.'

'I know. And you know what my job is. Don't try driving that taxi again today.'

'I told him,' the sister intoned.

They went back into the house and Jim had a cup of tea with them.

'Keeping you busy?' asked Roger, who had brightened, now that his whisky was gone and, with it, the worry whether or not to drink it. 'Anything interesting on?'

'Nothing great. Big charity man found dead in his hotel. Hotel deaths have to be looked into.'

'Oh, him. I had his wife in my cab the night it happened. Recognised her picture in the paper next day.'

Jim ceased stirring his tea. 'You're sure it was that night?'

'Positive. She was in quite a state. I realised why, when I read about it.'

'Roger, this might be important. Where did you drive Lady Lister?'

Roger laughed. 'Of all places, the Paradise Beach. None of my business, but I wouldn't have thought . . .'

'Was she alone?'

'Oh, sure.'

'Did you wait there for her? What happened?'

'Nothing. She paid me off and I came straight back. Lot of work that night. Big charity do on, at her hotel.'

'You've done me a turn, Roger. Maybe a big one.'

'I have? Well you did me one.' He beamed at his sister. 'See how Fate works out? If I hadn't had those couple of drinks . .'

She scowled and pointedly sloshed more tea into his cup.

Jim found Diana Lister at the Fort Regent conference centre. She walked straight over to him.

'Sergeant, I keep trying to speak to your superior, but he seems to be away.'

'Longer than he expected, Lady Lister. Can I help?'

'If you can authorise me to take my husband's body home. I do think this has gone on long enough. Mr Cassell will represent me at the rest of the conference.'

'Before you go any further,' Jim said, watching her eyes, 'you ought to know that I know you took a taxi to the Paradise Beach Hotel on the evening your husband died. The driver remembers the time, and says you were upset. Would you like to tell me about it?'

Her eyes fell and her shoulders sagged. She mumbled, 'Can we sit down somewhere – in the open air?'

He took her arm and guided her out on to a terrace where there were benches facing out over the harbour. She slumped down beside him, then turned to look at him with pleading eyes.

'Is it necessary? Really? It was natural causes.'

'I'm afraid it's got to be carried through. The doctor wasn't happy.'

She looked away again. 'It's so sordid. I can imagine the sort of things they'll write about him. I don't mind so much for my sake, but he did so much good. They'll drag his name through the mud, and it won't make the world a ha'porth better off.'

'I understand,' Jim said genuinely. 'I came near to dragging a young couple through it myself today. Luckily, I found they were in the clear. But it was all because of this same business, and because you weren't frank with us from the start. So, no more mysteries, please, Lady Lister, and we'll see how much further we might need to go, if at all.'

She nodded resignedly, and told him.

'I was just leaving the dinner when I was called to the telephone. It was some woman or girl. She didn't identify herself. She said Edward had been with her, and he'd had some sort of collapse, and she was afraid. She gave me the address and just rang off. I got a taxi straightaway and went

80

there. There was a young man on duty – Italian, I supposed. He pointed out a chalet.'

'Did he seem to know something had happened?'

'I was too flustered to notice. He didn't offer to go with me or anything.'

'Can you remember, when you spoke to him first, did you say you'd come to see Sir Edward Lister?'

'No. Definitely not. I was careful not to give my name, either. I just said I'd had a telephone call from a woman, asking me to come there.'

'And he seemed to know about it?'

'I think he must have done. He pointed out the chalet at once.'

'You didn't see the woman?'

'No. There was no one else.' She paused, as if having to muster her resources for a great effort. Then she went on.

'He was dead . . . in that horrible little room. Dead and . . . naked. His clothes were scattered about, it was so sordid – quite clear what had been . . .'

She paused again. Jim didn't try to prompt her.

'I'd always known about his affairs, though I'd pretended not to. Out of sight, out of mind, so far as it was possible for me. I never made the mistake of prying, or trying to find out who the women were. I'm sure they were all casual encounters – nothing likely to wreck our marriage. That would have been different.' There was a tinge of bitterness in her voice as she added, 'And, of course, nothing must ever hurt the precious Foundation. Anyway, I went back to the reception place and phoned Peter.'

'Mr Cassell?'

She nodded. 'I'm not sure that I could have got through these last days without him. Oddly enough, I'd always resented Peter. Ever since he joined my husband he'd pushed and pushed – more and more meetings, more conferences, travelling. The only blessing was that I could stay at home more, now that Edward had Peter to assist him everywhere. And he couldn't have been more thoughtful and kind to me when he came to that wretched place and saw for himself.'

'Was it his idea to move Sir Edward back to the hotel?'

'He said it was that or call the police. I couldn't. Not to that place. He was dead, a plain heart attack. That was enough to accept. I didn't want the scandal as well. I'd been protecting Edward and his wretched charity for fifteen years. It was automatic to want to hush it all up. Peter helped me dress the body. We took it back to the hotel in Edward's car, which was there. Between us we got him up the fire escape to Peter's room and then along to ours. It was the most squalid, sickening thing I've ever had to do.'

She dabbed her eye corners with the small handkerchief she had been clutching between her hands.

'And now, it seems, it was a wasted ordeal. Sergeant, you've your duty to carry out. Only . . . But, of course, you must do what's correct.'

She got up suddenly and walked, straight-backed and dignified, into the conference centre. Jim sat on for some minutes, staring seaward, concentrating his thoughts.

It seemed straightforward enough, if he believed her, and he did. She had not been frank with him until now, for the sake of her late husband's name. Cassell had not been open, either, probably for the same reasons. Jim wondered whether there was anything between the young clergyman and Lady Lister. It didn't seem likely.

Two people's testimony was left unaccounted for: the woman who had been in the bed with Lister when he had had his attack; and Nino Mandara who must know much more than he had admitted. The woman must have come to him, in her fright, and told him what had happened in the chalet. He would know that she had telephoned and then left hurriedly. He had directed Lady Lister to the chalet without comment or offer to help; and even if it hadn't been until next morning that he had found the watch, he was well aware from the inscription on it who the man in the chalet had been. Therefore, he had information to sell, in place of the price he might have got for the watch, and he seemed the type who might not hesitate to talk to any journalist willing to open his wallet.

He decided Nino needed warning off. He went down to the car park for his Triumph and drove to the Paradise Beach Hotel.

There was still no sign of life except in the reception area, where a paunchy, shifty-eyed man in his fifties was humping a crate of full beer bottles. He proved to be the manager.

'Bloody believe it!' the man grumbled. 'Ten days in Bermuda, me and the missus, and it rained all the bleeding time. Came down like bullets. We could've stayed here for the sun.'

'I'd like a word with Nino.'

'Bloody little Eytie. He's gone. Scarpered.'

Jim showed him his I/D card, saying, 'He can't have gone far. I've got his passport.'

'I know where you'll find him, mate. Club in St Helier where him and his kind hang out.'

'What exactly do you mean by "his kind"?'

The manager told him.

Driving into town, Jim concentrated his thoughts on Nino. Handsome little Nino, a camp follower at resorts where gentlemen with unorthodox tastes and enough money to indulge them could easily be found. Drop the word in a few hotel porters' ears. Promise them a percentage. Use a place where there could be no risk of interference or the client being recognised.

Nino, who had been cunning enough, after this partner had died on him, to gather up some fag ends from a bar ashtray he hadn't troubled to clear, an empty perfume spray he'd come across, a soiled tissue, and plant them all in the chalet, so that when the body was found and questions asked it would seem that a woman had been there. Lady Lister had said it had been a woman on the phone, telling her what had happened. Had it? Had Nino risked getting some real girlfriend to make the call? Or had he contrived the voice himself?

Jim knew the club well enough. The police left it alone. It was all so legal nowadays, and it was useful to know where men of their persuasion gravitated to, if any of them needed to be questioned.

He went in and saw Nino at once, talking to the middle-aged barman who was wearing make-up and who looked interestedly at the good-looking man approaching. Nino's expression was very different: all wariness. After fifteen minutes' questioning by Jim, at a table out of earshot of any other, his look was different still. When Jim left him, he left certain possibilities for him to ponder.

He went to the hotel and to Peter Cassell's room. The clergyman was working at documents, jacketless and in an open-necked shirt.

He greeted Jim solemnly. 'I hope you've come to tell me it's all cleared up and we can take Sir Edward home.'

'It's as good as settled. Has Lady Lister been in touch with you just recently?'

'She telephoned half an hour ago. She told me about her talk with you. I'm sorry I wasn't frank with you before, but we thought . . .'

'It could have saved a lot of trouble. I nearly dropped a couple of kids in it on your account.'

'I really am sorry.'

'They were Press, too. Could have raised all hell for you and her and your charity if I'd given them a whisper.'

'Well, yes. Lady Lister and I are most grateful to you personally, Sergeant. Obviously, you're a believer in live and let live.'

'Yes, I am. I'm also a believer in die and let's have an explanation of the dying. Suppose you give me the true one now.'

'But I thought Diana . . .'

'That was the one she'd have me believe is true. I'd like the one you know is true, Mr Cassell. It's everyone's day for being frank – Nino included.'

He saw Cassell's lips tighten and his head come up in surprise.

'He told me all of it,' Jim added. 'And, for my money, it was the only unexpurgated version I've heard.'

Cassell was silent for some moments. Then he said, 'Diana wasn't lying to you. She didn't know. She still doesn't.'

'That you were more to Sir Edward Lister than his assistant?'

'Yes. Soon after I came to work for him I discovered – we discovered – what he and I had in common. After that he wanted me everywhere with him. Diana resented having to travel so much for the charity, so she was happy to stay at home mostly while he and I went. I know she thought I was pushing him into too much travel, but it was just the opposite. He took on a lot more commitments, in order to be away with me. It's nothing I'm ashamed of, Sergeant Bergerac. It's an aspect of life that has been widely debated and accepted.'

'I know. You still haven't told me what happened, though.'

'Well, the fact is, while I was extremely fond of Edward, and grateful to him, I didn't like being monopolised, as he wanted. I'm a promiscuous person by nature. I wanted to be free to enjoy other friendships. Edward knew this, and objected very strongly. I told him that he must accept me the way I was. He said he couldn't and he sometimes went out of his way to keep a check on me.

'I'd heard of a club here in St Helier from friends in London. I went there while Edward and Diana were at a luncheon with the Lieutenant-Governor. I hadn't been invited, so I was free for a few hours. I met Nino. We were attracted, and . . .' He broke off with a dismissive shrug.

'He suggested the Paradise Beach?'

'Hardly my choice of place, but the manager and his wife were away and there were no guests. Nino was young, handsome . . . I arranged with him that I'd go there again on the evening of the dinner.'

'Surely you would have been expected to be at the dinner?'

'I asked Edward if he'd excuse me because I'd a lot of arrangements to make for next day. I don't know how he found where I'd gone, but, to cut it short, he arrived at the Paradise Beach in his car and burst in on Nino and me. He was almost screaming with fury. He went for Nino – literally threw himself at him – and . . .'

'That did it?'

'He collapsed. We tried everything – beating his chest, the kiss of life. Nothing worked. We were frightened. Nino said if I paid him well he'd phone the police and make out it had been Edward and he there alone. Even if I could have trusted Nino I couldn't allow that, for Diana's sake. I knew that she'd been putting up for years with Edward's philandering, but she'd always imagined it to be other women. To that extent, she'd accepted it. But to find . . . It was unthinkable.'

'It can complicate life, can't it, Mr Cassell?'

'We are as we are. Not everyone can accept it, though.'

'Wives in particular.'

'Obviously.'

'Well, I suppose it's marginally less of a shock to believe your husband died in bed with another woman, rather than a man.'

'Believe me, if I could have got him back to the hotel by myself, and made it appear he'd died in their room, I would have done. I wanted to spare Diana all I could, Sergeant.'

'And yourself.'

'I tell you, if I'd told her the truth it would have hurt her far more. If I'd telephoned the police from the Paradise Beach it would all have come out and she'd have learned the truth just the same. The only way was the one I tried, but we weren't clever enough. I suppose it all sounds callous and distasteful to you. Nino and I undressed Edward and put him on the bed and Nino got Diana to come there and find him.'

Jim had almost forgotten that the man watching him so anxiously was a clergyman. Amazing how a dog collar and black shirt front could change a man's aspect. But this wasn't the first time he'd been shown how different from their appearance people could turn out to be.

He got up.

'I'll play it the way you wanted it,' he said. 'For Lady Lister.'

'I'm very grateful to you.'

'Nino won't talk. I've put the fear of God into him – if

you'll pardon the expression. And you won't talk either, please, Mr Cassell. Ever, or I could lose my job.'

'I wouldn't dream of it.'

Jim left the hotel and went to the Bureau. Barney Crozier still wasn't back, it seemed, and all the day shift had gone home. He typed a report, taking two hours and several rewrites until he was satisfied with it. Then he got in his car and drove to the vineyard. As he got near it he found himself hoping Francine would be there. She wasn't.

He put on a recording of Elgar's First Symphony and listened to it with closed eyes. As always, it evoked shadowy images of Edwardian ladies moving across a sun-dappled lawn, against a dark background of cedar trees. This time, he distinctly recognised Francine amongst them.

Chapter Twelve

The morning hydrofoil slicing its way from St Malo to St Helier was full. Daytrippers, many of them French housewives in couples, carrying capacious shopping bags for the cheap purchases which would more than compensate for the price of the return fare.

There were a few tourists and a sprinkling of businessmen. One of them, aged about forty, with thinning hair and spectacles, was named Raymond Dumoiter. On boarding the craft he had gone straight to the bar area, furnished with couches and tables, and been the first to get his order taken by the fair-haired young steward, whose name was Simon Gibbins.

Another passenger, a man in his thirties, whose handsome looks were complemented by dark glasses and a black leather casual jacket, also made his way to the bar. All he ordered was an orange juice and he stood at the counter to sip it, though in such a position that he could keep Raymond Dumoiter in his sight. This last man was Jim Bergerac.

He had followed Dumoiter from Paris, to where he had tailed him from Jersey yesterday. He had kept close watch on him throughout. He had seen the meeting between Dumoiter and the Algerian behind a stall in the market in St Germaine. He had seen an exchange of what was obviously money for something else which he had not been able to see, though he was certain what it was. Now, while Dumoiter sat absorbed in the same copy of *Le Monde* which had occupied him on the train from Paris to St Malo, Jim watched him constantly.

They were only a few minutes from St Helier when Dumoiter finished his drink and went through to the toilet. Jim watched the door. As soon as Dumoiter came out he went in, ungallantly cutting off another passenger with the same intention. Jim's purpose was a different one, however. He searched the small compartment, looking to see if anything had been left tucked away there. He found nothing and came out, smiling at the impatient passenger who had been about to thump on the door. He leaned on the bar again and went on watching Dumoiter, who had been in his sight all morning.

Not quite, though. For a minute or two Dumoiter had been invisible to him, inside the toilet. For the next few minutes, Jim himself had been in there. And in that little extra time, Raymond Dumoiter had had his pocket picked, but didn't know it. Had Jim still been at his place he would probably have recognised the pickpocket's stumble against Dumoiter for what it was. But he had been out of view, searching; and what he had been looking for Dumoiter had now lost.

The squad pounced quickly when the hydrofoil had backed into its berth and Jim, amongst those who had got up on deck first, had sent a brief description of Dumoiter on his pocket-sized walkie-talkie. Barney Crozier was running the operation from an unmarked States Police car. A constable was with him and two others were in position, one in a plain van on the quayside, the other, dressed as a docker, on a crane. They were not quick enough for Dumoiter's instinct. He sensed them, noticing the 'docker' regarding him intently and seeing him wave to a man in the van, which began moving. Dumoiter started to run, encumbered by nothing more than a briefcase. Jim leaped ashore and went after him, as Crozier snapped an R/T order to the others and they converged.

Dumoiter knew that running would get him nowhere, literally, on this tiny island. They would certainly catch him before he could get off the quay. But he was buying what little time he could to give him a chance to throw away that which he knew made him the object of the chase. And as he fumbled for it in his pocket, he couldn't find it, because it was no longer there.

The realisation sent a chill wave of shock through him. But then the irony of it struck him, and he smiled and slowed down. When they caught him he made no more than the resistance of an innocent wayfarer who fears he is about to be mugged; and when they shoved an I/D card under his nose he stopped struggling entirely and asked innocently if they hadn't made some mistake . . . ?

They took him into a quayside office and searched him thoroughly – briefcase, pockets, socks, shoes. They turned his clothes inside out, looking for concealed hiding places. They found nothing.

'I told you, Inspector,' Dumoiter complained to Barney Crozier. 'You've got the wrong man.' He spoke in English. He was a native of Jersey.

'Oh no we haven't,' Jim Bergerac assured him. 'I was there in St Germaine market. I saw you meet the Algerian. I watched you do the exchange. I've watched you ever since.'

Dumoiter said smoothly, 'I remember you. You were at the bar all the time, boozing your way across.'

'Don't try pulling that one,' Jim said, hard. 'It was neat orange juice.' But he noticed Barney and the constable giving him a look. He was not going to live that down for a long while.

'I tell you,' Dumoiter was carrying on, sounding angry now, 'I am Raymond Dumoiter, of this Island. I am a respectable businessman. I deal in export/import – textiles, perfumes, leatherware . . .'

'Travelling back and forth to Paris regularly,' said Jim. 'The perfect cover for a drugs courier. We were tipped off by the Sûreté. I tell you, I saw you.'

'Well, they were wrong, and you need your eyesight testing. Now, Inspector, I want to call my wife. She'll be worried. And then I propose telephoning my lawyer. There's been a great mistake made, and someone's going to pay for it.'

'You'll have to wait,' replied Crozier grimly. 'We're going to search that hydrofoil from stem to stern before we let go of you. If it's not on you, you've hidden it on board.'

'Or I never had it – whatever "it" was.' Dumoiter grinned unpleasantly and began tying his shoes again as the others went out, leaving him under the constable's guard.

'You blew it,' Crozier told Jim bitterly as they crossed the quay.

'I didn't. He spotted you lot.'

'I mean before that. He either slipped it to another passenger to bring ashore for him, or he hid it, or he dumped it overboard.'

'I tell you it was none of those, Barney. I'd have seen him.'

'Well, he certainly didn't chuck it away, once he'd stepped ashore. One of us would have seen that.'

'Then what? It isn't on him. Where is it?'

They searched the hydrofoil in the vicinity where Dumoiter had been sitting, and went through the toilet minutely. They found nothing. They took Dumoiter back to the Bureau des Étrangers and reported to the Chief, who blew his top.

'A major drug haul, worth a hundred . . . two hundred thousand, maybe. Pushers, top man, the lot, it could have been. And what do we get? Nothing. Can't even pin it on the bloody messenger boy.'

'I saw him collect, Chief,' Jim insisted.

The Chief wasn't listening. He wasn't quick to anger, but he hammered his desk this time.

'I backed the Bureau all the way on this. Told the Sûreté we could handle it, because I didn't want their blokes cluttering up the scene and then grabbing all the credit. Now I have to explain to them and the States Committee that we mucked it up completely.'

'Shouldn't we put a tail on Dumoiter?' Jim suggested.

It was Crozier who answered. 'He won't go near the next bastard on the ladder. Be sure of that.' He sounded almost triumphant.

He left the room. The Chief regarded Jim for some moments, then said, his anger turned to regret, 'It won't help, you know, Jim.'

'Help what, sir?'

'When your review comes up. You know you're on fitness probation. If the medical board doesn't clear you completely there's not much I can do to get you the benefit of the doubt.'

91

Jim knew that. His board was tomorrow. He left the Chief's office determined to get a result by then. He didn't leave the Bureau premises immediately, though, but waited until he saw Dumoiter released, go home on foot. Then he followed him, crawling the Triumph.

Raymond Dumoiter's house was an elegant white Georgian one, in an expensive street whose residents had found cause to grumble in recent years at the building of a multi-storey car park which spoiled their outlook. It suited Jim, however. From the parking bay on the top level he had a clear view of Dumoiter's front door. A Range Rover was parked near it, but didn't obscure it. Jim settled down to watch and wait.

The beach of St Ouen's Bay, between the Atlantic surge and the plateau where the airport is laid out, is the Island's least populous. There are five unbroken miles of hard white sand from which to swim and surfboard, under the watch of a seasonal corps of beachguards, some recruited from Australia. It is also an excellent track for car racing.

Pop music beat out loudly from the sound centre which, with the garage and general shop, formed the beachfront complex proclaimed by a brash hoarding to be 'Bobby Carnegie's Grand Prix Jersey Motorcade'. Teenage youths and girls, magnetised to this place, hung about under the bunting, chewing and envying the racy sports cars and motorcycles for sale in the showroom. Their heads turned as one as, above the decibels of the music, they heard the wasp's whine of a sand-racing car coming fast along the beach.

Beside the chocolate-coloured Rolls-Royce, whose radio one of his mechanics was adjusting, Bobby Carnegie himself looked up to watch the car approaching. Carnegie, around forty, had fleshed out a lot since the photograph had been taken which adorned the hoarding. It showed him as a lean, good-looking young man, grimy-faced but grinning, perched on a racing car, winner's laurel wreath round his neck, squirting the inevitable bottle of champagne over an admiring crowd.

He had not been in the world championship class, but a frequent winner of major races on the mainland, until the law of averages had caught up with him and left him with one leg too mangled for him to operate a Formula One car with the requisite delicacy of touch. He had put his accumulated winnings and considerable hidden wealth into establishing this complex, and had prospered to a degree he had never imagined for himself when he had come from his native Scotland as a young mechanic. He had kept his accent, but now, instead of overalls, it went with an expensively cut white linen suit, handmade open-necked shirt, gold watch and bracelet and gold pendant on a chain round his neck. He leaned on a stout stick.

The man he had been chatting with looked up also. This was Sam Tirrell, Carnegie's hard-muscled assistant and confidant on all matters.

The teenagers thrilled as the custom-built racing car roared past in a blur, already beginning to slow towards the distant point where it turned exaggeratedly and came back to the complex, sprinkling sand off its wheels.

Tirrell walked away towards the office, to answer the telephone, as his employer limped to the side of the car and put out his hand to receive the white crash helmet and face shield from the clearly elated driver, who was Charlie Hungerford. Charlie climbed out of the tight cockpit and started to strip off the white overalls.

'Still a wee tiger in your tank, Charlie,' said Carnegie.

'Touched a hundred and ten,' Charlie said proudly. 'Haven't had so much fun for years.'

'Can I sell you one, then?'

'At my age?'

'No age limit in the Channel Trophy.'

'Twenty years ago, maybe,' Charlie replied, smoothing down his grey hair. 'The old blood pressure wouldn't stand it now, even if my bank account could.'

Carnegie grinned at him, well aware that he was talking to a millionaire with his hands on enough money to keep half-a-dozen banks respectful.

'Good of you to let me have a go,' Charlie said. 'Ever take a spin yourself these days?'

Carnegie lifted his stick. 'I don't want to end up with two of these. This place takes up all my time, anyway.'

'Looks a good business. What do I owe you?'

'Buy me a drink at the club next time.' A blare of sound from the Rolls interrupted him. 'Looks as if your radio's fixed, and I see I'm wanted on the phone. Be in touch, Charlie.'

The ex-racer limped briskly away to his office, in response to Sam Tirrell's urgent wave. Tirrell was back at the telephone, holding a hand over the mouthpiece, looking anxious.

'Our delivery man. Picked up by the cops. He was clean and they let him go.'

'Clean?' Carnegie raised an eyebrow. 'How could he be?'

Tirrell shrugged. His boss took the telephone from him and said simply, 'Yes?'

He listened for a few moments, then said slowly, 'That's what you certainly need to do – explain. This evening, eight, same place you met Sam last time.'

He hung up without waiting for any acknowledgment. As he turned from it his eyes were as hard and narrowed as they had been the last time he had battled it out along the home straight at Le Mans at over a hundred with a Frenchman and a Swede fighting him for first past the flag, and had ended up pinned under his overturned car.

Chapter Thirteen

It was possible that Jim's vigil could prove a long one. He had a date with Francine for luncheon at the Royal Barge and by the time noon came he knew he wasn't going to make it. The elderly traffic warden on car park duty was an ex-PC named Brooks. Doing his rounds and seeing Jim in the parked car he had come over and chatted. He appeared again and Jim called him over, to ask him to do him a favour and make a telephone call. He wrote the message down and the old man left him to it.

Francine was sipping a Pernod and chatting lightly with Diamanté Lil at the Royal Barge's bar. The call came through to her there. Her eyes widened as she listened to Warden Brooks's message. She had to muster some courage to relay it to Lil, who in turn passed it to Gulliver, who looked grimmer still. All the same, he did as Jim had requested. An hour later, Francine was sitting beside him in the Triumph, eating a gourmet meal in take-away style from plastic boxes and with a half-bottle of wine for her and a Perrier for him perched on the dashboard.

He had told her why he couldn't leave his post, and described the morning's disaster and its implications. She understood; she admired his dedication. All the same, she was disappointed. It had been her intention, over dinner at the Barge, to tell him of the decision she had made. Instead, she told him it here in the car park, while he kept his eyes on Dumoiter's house.

'I've given my notice to the Tourism Office, Jim. My mother wants me to go home to Cherbourg. She's a widow, and she needs me to help with my young brother and sister.'

He flicked her a glance, and she recognised his reaction.

'I'm sorry, Frankie.'

95

'But you can stay on at the vineyard. I've spoken to my friends.'

'Thanks. I suppose things aren't the same – without Tom.'

'It isn't that. That's over.'

'Good. When do you leave?'

'In a few days. I have to sort out things at the apartment I've been sharing.'

'You never asked me round there.'

'No. I'll miss Jersey.'

'I'll miss you. And your English will go to rack and ruin.'

She smiled. 'Just when I was beginning to understand the jokes.'

They continued eating. As a change of subject it occurred to her to ask, 'By the way, when you searched the hydrofoil did you find anything at all? I mean, besides what you were looking for?'

'Not a thing. The usual litter normally tidy people seem to think it proper to scatter in public transport. Why?'

'We had a Frenchman in the office. He'd just got into town from the hydrofoil and realised he'd lost his purse. You know how Frenchmen carry purses. He asked us to telephone the ferry office to ask if it had been found. The girl said the steward had not reported it and no one had handed it in. We advised the man to go to the police, but he said he had his return ticket and his credit cards safe in a separate case, and he preferred to get on with his shopping rather than sit around a police station all day. We took his name and address and promised to send it to him if it is found.'

'Can't help, I'm afraid. He was quite sure he'd lost it actually on board?'

'Positive. He had paid for a cup of coffee with a note from it, and put it carefully back in the usual pocket. We French take care of our money, you know.'

'No comment. Perhaps there was one of the light-fingered brigade aboard, coming over ready for the season's business. It's worth their while coming thousands of miles to a busy tourist place, you know. The Australians and South Americans have it organised in gangs.'

He was chatting, merely, not giving the notion of a pickpocket any serious thought. Anyway, he would have noticed any passenger moving round amongst the rest in a suspicious way. His mind returned to Francine.

'Will I see you again?' They had finished the meal and she was gathering up the debris to take to a litter bin.

'I hope so. I must move my things from the vineyard, and I have to work out this week for my notice.'

'Dinner, then? To make up for today. A promise.'

She smiled at him. 'Yes, please.'

'I'll be in touch.'

There was the briefest hesitation on both their parts before she opened the door and got out. He almost put a hand out to draw her to him to kiss her. She almost waited for him to do it. The hesitation killed it, and he made no move. Francine got out quickly and went, bearing the empty cartons. He forced himself not to watch her, but to keep his eyes on Dumoiter's front door.

It proved to be a long wait indeed. He had had no sleep the night before, and on top of that the concentration required to follow and watch Dumoiter all the way from Paris to St Helier. Often that afternoon he felt his eyelids dropping, fighting them apart. He realised that the rich alfresco meal had been a mistake, leaving him even drowsier. Three times Warden Brooks brought him reviving mugs of tea; but he wondered how long he could keep up the watch. He thought of getting Brooks to phone Crozier to send a relief. That would be giving in, though. If nothing happened he would be blamed for wasting the Bureau's resources. If anything did, and he wasn't there to follow it up, he risked missing out on credit he badly needed.

It was seven o'clock before it happened, and the sudden flood of adrenalin worked as effectively as a bucketful of cold water. The front door of the house opened. Dumoiter came out alone. He closed the door and went to the Range Rover, standing by it to select the key to its door.

The little time it took him to climb in, start up and give the engine a few revs from cold were enough for Jim to start his own car, back swiftly, and go spiralling down the car park's ramps. It was a pay-and-display park, so there was no barrier to hold him up, and, thankfully, no dawdling car ahead. He shot out of the exit in time to see the Range Rover turn a corner, and he accelerated after it.

They passed through a road tunnel and then headed eastwards along the coast road flanking St Aubin's Bay. Jim could afford to keep well back without risk of losing the Range Rover, until it turned abruptly into a minor road leading inland. Although it is so small, the Island has over five hundred miles of road, and not even a member of the States Police could be expected to anticipate a driver's destination, heading away from the coast. Jim was forced to risk closing up and showing his car in Dumoiter's rear mirror from time to time, rather than lose him.

He thought he had lost him at one point. A straight stretch of road lay ahead, but with no sign of the Range Rover on it. The only turning was a short driveway up to the gates of grounds and on towards a bulky group of stone buildings. Jim slowed and drove past. The Range Rover was just being admitted to the grounds by the lodgekeeper, who wore a brown habit and evidently knew Dumoiter well, for he was smiling up at him. The heavy gate which the man swung shut behind the Range Rover bore the sign FRANCISCAN BROTHERS OF ST MARTIN.

Jim found a turning place a little further on and drove back to within some fifty yards of the lodge and gates. He switched off the engine and resigned himself to another wait. The anti-climax of it, after the welcome activity, made it even harder for him to keep his eyes open. After a half-hour's struggle he started the car again, drove up to the gates, and held out his I/D card to the lay brother who came from the lodge. The man returned him a benign smile and admitted him without question.

Jim motored up the curving drive to the monastery buildings. A bell was tolling thinly. He could see nothing of Dumoiter's vehicle. He parked near an open doorway and walked in. Apart from the faint bell continuing distantly there was a stony silence. He found himself stepping lightly, trying not to disturb it.

Several doors off the hall were open, though there seemed to be no one in any of the rooms. Perhaps they were all bidden to some service by the bell. The visiting Dumoiter as well? What had he done with the Range Rover?

One of the rooms, a little larger than the others, interested Jim enough to attract him into it. It was a laboratory, simply equipped with a sink, some benches, and an assortment of bottles, retorts on stands, a centrifuge and racks of test tubes, many of them containing colourless fluids. He went to the bottles and took the lid off one containing white powder, to sniff the contents.

'Just a moment!' a voice called sharply behind him. He turned, to see a tall friar, gaunt and almost completely bald, approaching.

'I shouldn't touch that,' the friar said, in a cultivated voice. 'It's dangerous. Acid.'

'Acid?' Jim echoed, taking the word at its contemporary meaning.

'For our work here. I'm Brother Matthias. Who are you?'

Jim got his card out again. The friar glanced at it and made a humorous grimace.

'Come to check up on the purity of our product, have you?'

'What's that, sir?'

'Perfume. Well, the essence, at any rate. We make it from the Jersey Lily. We don't put in the pong, though. That's a much more sophisticated process. They do it in Paris, from musk and whale sperm and that sort of thing.'

The mention of Paris brought Jim sharply back to his purpose.

'Do you know Mr Raymond Dumoiter?' he asked.

'Of course. He's our agent. He takes the essence over and sells it for us.'

'Well, perhaps you can tell me where I can find him? I saw him drive in half-an-hour ago. I've been waiting by the gate.'

'Ah, then you've missed him. He merely popped in to

report that he had delivered our last consignment safely and to pass on the manufacturer's compliments on its quality.'

'I was at the gate.'

'Raymond said he would leave by the flower garden gate at the back. He always appreciates our flowers.'

Jim restrained himself from profanities – verbal ones, at least – until he had got off that holy territory, driving back the way he had come. He was certain now that Dumoiter had noticed that he was being tailed. It was pointless driving about in the hope of picking him up again. In any case, he reflected, there was nothing more he could have said to him. The illicit errand he had been expecting had been an innocent one after all, as the friar had verified. Jim realised that exhaustion had blurred his judgment. He should never have gone in; but, having done so, it was as well that he had not found Dumoiter, who might not have been aware precisely who was on his track.

As he went through St Helier he made a point of passing Dumoiter's house. There was no sign of the Range Rover. It could be anywhere on the island by now, and he was in no state to go searching for it. He drove to the vineyard. Francine wasn't there. He didn't care. He threw off his clothes, fell into bed, and was asleep before he had pulled the sheet round his shoulders.

Chapter Fourteen

Gulliver was checking his lobster pots on the beach at L'Étacq not long after daybreak next morning when it began to rain wallets and purses. He had never known it rain either wallets or purses before, let alone both together, so he scrambled up the overhang of rocks which had hidden him from the clifftop above, the better to investigate the phenomenon.

He saw a battered old Volkswagen Beetle chugging away and got a glimpse of its driver, a fair-haired young man whom he thought he knew, but couldn't immediately put a name to.

The little chef climbed down again and picked up the objects which had come scattering into the shallow water and would soon have been washed away if he had not been there to retrieve them.

The purses were completely empty. One of the wallets had some credit cards in it, the other some odd papers. There was no cash. Gulliver took them to the police.

They were on Charlotte's desk in the Bureau when Jim came in a few hours later. Charlotte thought how dejected he looked. She knew his medical board was due late that afternoon, and guessed how apprehensive that must be making him. She had heard about the abortive attempt to catch the drug courier with the goods on him. Putting the two together made it not hard to read his expression accurately.

He was feeling physically better for the long, deep sleep, with none of the hangover effects from the bad old days to follow it. But his first waking thought had been that his trail after Dumoiter had gone stone cold and the man would be too watchful to give him another go at him. The second had been that it was the make-or-break day of his medical.

The third was that Francine was leaving; and that, to his surprise, troubled him more than the others did.

Charlotte noted the change of expression which the sight of the unaccustomed objects on her desk produced. Without his having to ask, she told him how Gulliver had brought them in to the police, who had recognised them as obviously belonging to visitors and thankfully passed them, and the buck, to the Bureau.

'This is the one that'll interest you,' she said, handing over the wallet with the credit cards in it. 'Raymond Dumoiter's.'

He grabbed it eagerly and searched it though finding nothing else. He sniffed hard at its inside.

'Has Barney seen this yet?' he asked.

'You're the first in.'

He winked at her and stuck Dumoiter's wallet in his pocket and hurried out, looking a great deal more cheerful than a few moments earlier. He left the building without running into Barney Crozier or any of the other Bureau detectives, and roared off in the Triumph towards the Royal Barge.

The scent of coffee was delicious on the air. Gulliver and Diamanté Lil were sitting drinking it and eating buttered croissants and jam, she in a revealing silk embroidered negligée, he in his chunky oiled wool sweater and Wellingtons. Lil brought a cup for Jim and poured, and Gulliver pushed croissants towards him. He didn't refuse them, letting them melt lingeringly in his mouth while Gulliver told him of his extraordinary harvest from the sea.

'An old banger,' he said of the car. He was not a car fancier. 'One of those ugly German things.'

'Beetle?'

'Something like that.'

Lil rolled her eyes at Jim.

'You didn't get the number, by any chance?' he asked.

'Didn't think.'

'He can't even read the menu board,' Lil said.

'I can cook it, though,' the little chef retorted.

'But you got a glimpse of the driver,' Jim prompted.

'Lad about twenty. Fair hair. Something about him . . . And the car . . . orange colour. Can't get it, but I've seen them before.'

Lil said, 'We've been running through our younger customers, but we haven't worked it out.'

'I can ask around the garages,' Jim said.

'Garage! That's it,' cried Gulliver. 'Filling station at St Aubin. The boy used to work there.'

Jim denied himself the pleasure of one more croissant in his haste to get to the place. The proprietor's wife, masculine-looking in dungarees and a baseball cap, reached out her hand for the pump nozzle, but he shook his head.

'You mean Simon,' she said, when he had explained. 'Simon Gibbins.' The name was clearly distasteful to her. 'Don't talk to me about *him!*'

'I'd be glad if you would to me, though.'

'In trouble, is he? Doesn't surprise me. D'you know, five years ago his mother used to swan about in an American four-wheel drive. Great flash thing. Came in here two or three times a week, it used so much gas. And she had a Porsche for swanking out to dinner in. The pools, that was it. Best part of two hundred thousand. Spent the lot – drank it, rather. And next thing he's round here begging for a job. Couldn't say no, could we, after his mum'd spent a fortune with us? Wish we had. You'd think he was out to get it all back, overcharging and pocketing the extra. Lost us customers. My old man wouldn't bring charges, because he reckoned it'd be more trouble than it was worth. Gave him the push, though. I've had to work the pumps myself ever since. You don't want any petrol? That poor old thing looks thirsty to me.'

'Love to oblige,' Jim grinned, 'but I filled her up first thing. Where does the boy live, d'you know?'

'With his mum, then. Don't know about now. Big Spanish house at Grouville, called "Three Crosses".'

Jim thanked her and started his engine.

'Should have been "Double Cross", more like,' she said.

He gave her another grin and zoomed away.

It was not yet ten o'clock in the morning, but Gloria Gibbins was already at work topping up the booze in her veins from the night before. Jim felt no disgust. He had been down that road, though not quite so far. But Alcoholics Anonymous members didn't go around evangelising. They minded their own business until people saw fit to approach them.

She would have been attractive in her day, he saw, but that day was almost irretrievably past. She was in her late forties with straggly blonde-dyed hair, no make-up, and a drinker's puffy skin. She wore a stained T-shirt and frayed jeans and had grubby bare feet. She lay on a sun-lounger beside a neglected swimming pool on her unswept terrace. The pool had no water in it, only leaves. She was propping a wineglass on her stomach.

'He's a big grown boy,' she replied to Jim's question. 'I don't ask him how he spends his time.'

'Perhaps you ought to, Mrs Gibbins.'

'The hell with them! Their filthy language and their loud music. I don't want his friends coming swarming here.'

'You care about Simon, though.'

She looked at him with dulled eyes between spongy lids.

'I'm his mother. Ask him if he cares for me – always going off.'

'Where does he go?'

She didn't answer, but, with some effort, struggled off the couch and stood up unsteadily. She noticed his glance at the glass she held.

'More refreshing than coffee,' she said. 'Have a glass?'

He shook his head. She picked her way deliberately into the house through the French windows, as though she were walking on powdered glass. Jim followed her into the untidy lounge, a big room with furnishings which must have been bought regardless of cost or harmony. The only pictures on the walls were framed photographs of scenes of revelry, in which he could recognise Mrs Gibbins. If they had been taken no more than five years ago, she had certainly deteriorated fast.

He was surprised to see one of her being hugged cheek-to-cheek by Charlie Hungerford. They had champagne glasses in their hands and streamers round their necks.

'Simon might be in trouble,' he tried again. She was refilling her glass from a two-litre bottle of white wine. She ignored his remark. He tried instead, 'How do you know Charlie Hungerford, Mrs Gibbins?'

This produced a reaction. 'Charlie? A right one he is. They all used to come round here, the millionaires. Charlie, Beresford, Vance, Andrew Wilson – I knew them all. Friend of yours, too, is he?'

'My ex-father-in-law.'

She sipped and looked at him with curiosity.

'So it was you who married snobby Debby. I like Charlie, even if he does like to play the big cigar. She was a stuck-up teenager. Found you didn't fit in, eh?'

'Not really my scene.'

'Mine while I had what it took. Money attracts money. They all came flocking here. Then they all went away again.'

She drank off the glass at a swallow and refilled it.

'It doesn't help – in the end,' he said gently but pointedly.

'No need to tell me what I know,' she answered, but refilled the glass.

'Your son . . .' he tried again.

'I wish you'd leave off about him.'

'I told you, he may be in trouble – real trouble. You said he's always going off. Do you know where?'

She slumped down on to the sofa, patting the space beside her. He ignored the hint. The combination of drink, disillusion and loneliness was as potentially deadly in a once-attractive woman at ten a.m. as at any other time.

'I need to know,' he insisted.

She made a sulky mouth. 'The damned hydrofoil.'

Jim suddenly had that feeling of the clues slotting together. 'Where does he go?' he asked.

'For Christ's sake, St Malo and back! Where else?'

'When would the last time have been, d'you know?'

He thought she might have thrown the wine at him in her exasperation, but she drank some of it instead.

'Today. Yesterday. Every day. He works on it.'

Jim's memory swept the faces of the crew. He couldn't place a fair-haired boy of about twenty. Then he remembered the steward.

'I want to talk to Simon, Mrs Gibbins. You'll be doing him a favour, and yourself, as well as me, if you'll get him to ring the Bureau and ask for me as soon as you see him again. It might save him getting hurt.'

She was looking at him contemptuously, her eyes half-closed.

'I'll tell you something,' she said thickly. 'Charlie Hungerford may be a bastard, but he's more fun than his ex-bloody-son-in-law.'

Jim turned and left by the French window.

He drove to the Bureau. Charlotte gave him an apprehensive look when he came into the outer office, where she was typing. Barney Crozier's door was wide open. His voice and the Chief's were raised in argument.

'You,' Charlotte whispered.

Jim braced himself and went through.

They ceased talking as he came in. Crozier was standing behind his desk, the Chief beside it.

'You're in it now, all right,' Crozier told Jim. He was red with fury up to his receded hair line.

'What have I done?' Jim asked, trying to think of something. Gloria Gibbins surely couldn't be far enough gone to have pulled the old attempted rape accusation?

'You know damn well,' Barney said. 'Couldn't stand him giving you the slip, could you? Had to go and beat hell out of him for it.'

'Just what are you on about, Barney?' Jim retorted; but he was already beginning to realise it.

The Chief answered, more quietly. 'Dumoiter has lodged a complaint against you. He says you followed him in your car when he was on a legitimate business errand. You laid in wait for him and got hold of him and beat him up.'

'You believe that, Chief?' said Jim bitterly.

'He showed us the cuts and bruises. They're real. Not the sort you can do to yourself, either.'

106

'Well, he's lying. Yes, I did follow him. I watched his house then went after him in his Range Rover in the evening. He went to the Franciscan monastery of St Martin. I waited half an hour, but he sold me a dummy.'

'What did you want him for?'

'I didn't want him. I wanted to see where he would go, who he'd meet. I wanted to know who he'd have to explain to that he'd lost the drugs he was bringing them, and what they'd do to him for it. Then we'd have identified the lot of them. Look, if you want to check up, give the monastery a ring. Ask for Brother Matthias. He talked to me. He told me about Dumoiter.'

'You told him Dumoiter was a suspect?' Crozier almost shouted.

'Don't be a bloody fool, Barney. I didn't tell him anything except that I wanted a word with Dumoiter. I had to give some excuse for going in there looking for him. I played it down.'

'All right. And then you chased after Dumoiter?'

'I didn't. I went back home. To the vineyard. I was knackered after watching all day and no sleep the night before. I went out like a light till this morning.'

'Anyone corroborate that?' Crozier asked snidely, making Jim wonder whether he'd noticed that he and Francine were seeing a good deal of one another.

'Nobody. I was alone.'

The Chief said unhappily, 'Dumoiter's laid an official complaint, Jim. His bruises are real. We're forced to accept his word.'

'Against mine!'

'Till it can be investigated. He's got grievance enough against us already, getting grabbed and being found clean.'

Crozier said, 'See it the way the Senator's bound to. First you screw it up at the hydrofoil . . .'

'*I* screwed it up!'

'Then you take things into your own hands out of revenge.'

'You believe that?' Jim rasped. He tore Dumoiter's wallet from his pocket and flung it on to the desk top with a slap.

'That's what he was carrying the stuff in. He didn't have it on him when he landed because it was nicked from him on board. That and some other passengers' things over the last trip or two. The guy who nicked them got rid of them over the clifftop at L'Étacq early this morning. I've got a witness who saw him and his car, and I think I know who he was. As for Dumoiter's richly-deserved bruises, my bet is they were done by his masters when he met them last night. Either to teach him a lesson for being careless, or because they suspect he's got the stuff stowed away somewhere, waiting to cash in on it for himself. I don't think he has. I think the dip who took his wallet has it, and he's an amateur who may get his head torn off if they get to him before I can.'

'You're off the case,' Crozier snapped.

Jim stared at him, then at the Chief, who said, 'I'm sorry. You know the rules, Jim. A formal complaint must be investigated.'

'Thank *you!*'

'Jim, don't go over the top now. You have this medical coming up. It's touch and go for you already. Give Barney the evidence you think you have, and he'll follow it up.'

'I haven't any. Just a set of suspicions and hunches of my own.'

'Well, go away and think about them,' Crozier said. 'If you come up with anything you think I might buy, come and tell me.'

'You wouldn't want to know, Barney. Your mind's closed, where I'm concerned.'

Jim moved to the door, only pausing to add, 'But I want *this* on record for your investigation. I haven't laid a finger on Dumoiter – yet!'

He stormed out, past Charlotte and out of the building.

Chapter Fifteen

He went to the Health Club, a multi-purpose establishment catering for those who wanted to work at getting and keeping fit, those who merely enjoyed squash followed by a sauna, and those purely social members who liked to sit over a pot of good tea in the relaxing lounge.

He made for the gymnasium where there was a bicycling machine. He set the gear to minimum pressure and for several minutes pedalled at an unflagging pace which, theoretically, would have carried him half the length of the entire island. The injured leg stood it perfectly. The last thing he intended to happen to him was to fail that medical.

When he had showered and dried himself off he went through to the tea lounge, where he was hailed by Charlie Hungerford, wearing a towelling robe and with a squash racquet propped against his chair. He was taking tea with a burly man who obviously did not play squash and who was wearing casual outdoor clothes.

'Cup of tea?' Charlie offered, giving Jim his crocodile smile.

'Wouldn't mind,' he nodded. A word with his ex-father-in-law would quite suit him, if the other man would buzz off. If Charlie had been close with Gloria Gibbins he might know something about her son.

'Do you know Bobby Carnegie?' Charlie said, as Jim sat and the other man nodded a greeting. He recognised Carnegie's name. He had once seen him drive in a race, but apart from his picture in the papers several years ago he had never seen his face, although it seemed vaguely familiar. He remembered there had been an accident, and noticed the thick stick against Carnegie's chair.

'Jim Bergerac,' he introduced himself. 'Bureau des Étrangers.' They shook hands across the table.

Charlie had beckoned a steward to fetch an extra cup and saucer. He poured for Jim.

'Bobby's just been telling me about some quack in Paris who treated his leg. Might do yours some good.'

'It's fine, thanks. You're in the car and stereo business now, aren't you?' Jim said to Carnegie.

Charlie answered for him. 'Man after my own heart, Bobby. Into anything where there's a chance of a decent return.'

Carnegie winked at Jim. 'You ever want anything in my line, come over and see me. Any friend of Charlie's will get a good deal.'

'He means you'll pay twice as much as anywhere else,' Charlie jested. 'He's as bent as his Harry Lauder stick.'

'You've just reminded me to bill you for fixing your Rolls's radio,' Carnegie grinned, getting up. 'See you again, Bergerac.'

He limped away, depending a lot on the stick's support.

'Good man, Bobby,' said Charlie. 'Let me take one of his sand-racers out. Great experience. You should try it.'

'Speaking of great experiences, Charlie, what about Gloria Gibbins?'

'Gloria? You know her?'

'I was at her house. We were talking about you.'

'Old gossip, then. I haven't seen her for long enough. Gone downhill, hasn't she?'

'A fair way, yes. Misses her old friends, it seems.'

'Easy come, easy go, Jim. Used to have some great times with her before the silly woman spent it all.'

'That put her beyond the pale, did it?'

Charlie shrugged. 'You put it together, you've got to keep it that way if you want to stay in the swim. But you never wanted to be in it, did you?'

Jim ignored the gibe. 'How about her son, Simon?'

'Hardly knew him. I didn't go to Gloria's for family gatherings. What about him?'

'Nothing. I just wondered if he might be a friend of any friends of yours.'

110

'Not unless he's in business and smart at it.'

'I think he's in business, but I don't know how smart. Thanks for the tea, Charlie. How's Deborah?'

'Surviving.'

'Tell her I'll fix a day with Kim as soon as I've got something out of the way.'

'Will do.'

From the Health Club Jim went down to the ferry office, to ask them to get Simon Gibbins to contact him when he came back with the hydrofoil. They told him it was Simon's day off, but, no, they'd no idea where he might be. Gloria had said he was working. Jim doubted that he kept her very informed of his movements, but it certainly implied that he wasn't at home.

He got back into his car and drove, slowly and methodically, searching St Helier for a battered orange Volkswagen Beetle. He didn't find it, however, for the place where it was parked was away from a road, near a quiet beach some distance from the town. Drawn up on the beach was a small boat, and in the boat, in close embrace, were Simon Gibbins and a girl in her late teens named Stella.

At length, they sat up. Stella wriggled her mini-skirt down from around her waist and tugged the T-shirt back from her shoulders, where he had pushed it up. She was thin and pale, with a punk-dyed hairdo; but when she spoke it was with a cultivated accent.

'I'd forgotten how much I fancied you. Where have you been these weeks?'

'Working. You?'

She shrugged. 'Around. My parents don't like people like me dirtying their Belcroute doorstep. They'd approve of you – nice boy, earning a living.'

He was fastening his jeans. He said casually, 'You could earn one.'

'How? On my back? I don't go for it that much. You're privileged.'

'I don't mean that way. If you'd do a job for me – an errand – there'd be a good cut in it for you and something to make you dazzle.'

111

She looked at him sharply.

'You having me on?'

'No.'

'You're not . . . dealing?'

'Why not? Others do well enough out of it.'

'What is it – coke? Where the hell did you get that sort of money?'

'I didn't.'

'Jeez, Simon, don't tell me you nicked it.'

Her eyes were wide. He grinned. 'Let's say it sort of fell out of a bloke's pocket on the way from St Malo.'

'A delivery man! They'll slaughter you if they find you.'

'How will they?'

'If you start dealing they'll soon know some of their regulars aren't buying suddenly. It won't take much working out.'

He said stubbornly, 'Look, I've got the stuff – a lot of it. I'm not handing it back. It's worth too much, and money I want, not just small change out of purses. You've got the contacts, Stella. You've got your supplier. Act as go-between for me and you'll have enough to tell your folks to take a running jump.'

'I . . . I wouldn't dare. He'd be suspicious. He'd start asking questions – where I'd got the stuff from . . .'

'All you tell him is you have this friend who's got a supply. You don't know any more except your friend's looking for a deal. You know how the stuff turns up on this island sometimes. Some amateur brings some in, some small-time dealer looking for a connection. If you must give any answers, say your friend's a businessman over in Jersey for a conference. You've promised not to identify him . . .'

She was hesitating now, moistening her colourless lips, tempted.

He reached into his pocket.

'I brought a sample for you,' he said. 'Thought you might like to try the quality. Do you want it, or do I have to chat up someone else?'

She had never had any offered her free before – except the

112

first time, when it had been bait to get her on the hook. The hook had gone well and truly in, and she had long since ceased fighting it.

'OK,' she said. 'Dazzle me.'

Simon watched the euphoria take over. He had never been tempted himself. He didn't even drink. His mother's example had been enough to keep him off that, and he regarded drug-taking as the same sort of disease, practised on the Island by rich kids who thought it trendy but could take it or leave it, and by the punks and drop-outs like Stella, who had no incentive to leave off and whose whole existence had become geared to raising the money for the supplier's next visit.

He drove her back to the open air public swimming pool where he had picked her up. She got out, pulled her man's jacket over her shoulders, and walked dazedly over to the wall where other punks of both sexes drooped and lolled and the pop music blared. Then Simon drove home. She was happily away now, capable of doing what he had asked without having to act a part. She would telephone him when it was done.

His mother was asleep on her lounger, an empty bottle and glass down beside her. He regarded her with a mixture of disgust and pity. She wasn't the first big pools winner to have proved unable to cope, especially after losing the lot and her husband as well. What Simon earned and stole was about all they had coming in, and he dared not thieve on the hydrofoil too often. He did some of it on shore, where tourists thronged. He had been taught by a French professional, who had complimented him on his skill and stolen the watch off Simon's wrist as a farewell gesture.

Gloria opened her eyes suddenly and saw him there.

'How long've you been home?' she asked through slack lips. 'What . . . what time is it?'

'Does it matter?' He found contempt hard to suppress.

'There was a policeman here. Looking for you.'

It alarmed him, but he didn't let her see it.

'Me? Why me?'

'He thinks you might be in trouble. Wants to help. *Are* you, Simon?'

'Hell no. Everything's fine.'

'Is it?' She knew about his stealing. He openly shared the spoils with her. She hated it, but the booze had to be paid for with something. 'I wish you wouldn't steal any more. You're bound to get caught. The sooner this house is sold, the better.' It was heavily mortgaged and there were other loans set off against it, but she clung to the notion that it would solve everything. Her lawyer was currently looking into the prospects for a sale.

Simon sat on the terrace wall. 'You may not need to sell it,' he told her, with an enigmatic smile.

She had struggled up to a half-sitting posture.

'What are you talking about?'

He had already been up to his room and got from its hiding place the slim black plastic pouch he had found in the unknown passenger's wallet. He held it up.

'This. Bonus pickings.'

'What is it? I can't see.'

'Coke. Cocaine.'

'Oh, no!'

'Calm down. The man I lifted it off must've been smuggling it in. He won't be reporting it to the coppers.'

'You've got to hand it in. Anonymously, I mean. Post it to them. Get rid of it somehow.'

'Like hell! Don't you realise what it means? A bloody fortune. Our salvation. All I have to do is sell it . . .'

'You mustn't. It's wicked. Immoral.'

'Any more than that poison you pour down your throat? There are plenty of kids ready to pay for it. How they use it's their affair.'

'You don't really believe that, Simon. Not you.'

'What I believe is that we need a way out, and this is it. It'll fetch enough to pay for everything. We won't be sold up and thrown off the Island. You can have the house done up, water in the pool again, your old cronies will come flocking back . . .'

'Simon, that policeman – Sergeant Bergerac – he said you might be in danger. Perhaps he knows about this already.'

'He can't know about anything. If he thinks he does, he can't prove it. Perhaps he suspects I've nicked a few bob. Someone's reported a lost purse too many. He wanted to scare you into warning me off.'

'I *am* scared now Bloody scared!'

'Forget it. Forget I told you about this.' He got down from the wall. 'You can save your thanks till after it's sold.' He began to move away.

'Please!' she called. 'He says you're in danger and he wants to help. He said to get you to call him . . .'

'I don't suppose you know what he said,' Simon replied, and went.

It was what people of more conventional habits termed lunchtime when Sam Tirrell came down to the open air swimming pool. The kids who sagged there, round-backed and empty-eyed, observed no formal intervals between the hours. Time for them was measured by Sam Tirrell's visits, and their only hunger was for the provisions he brought.

He usually came alone. His boss, Bobby Carnegie, preferred to keep his distance from the trade which brought him in money far exceeding what he made from selling cars and stereos; more than the rich pickings of his racing days. He paid Sam well to do the dirty work of pushing the pot and speed and coke. Tirrell wouldn't grass if he got caught. He knew Bobby would look after him so long as he kept his mouth shut, but that it would be more than his life was worth to open it.

Today, though, Carnegie watched from a distance in a car: an anonymous, mass-production model no one would think of associating with the prosperous ex-racer, whose tastes were for the latest in styling and power.

Today was different because, in spite of the beating Tirrell had given him, Raymond Dumoiter had stuck to his story that his pocket had been picked. They knew he had no guts

115

and would not have gone on taking the blows if he had had a truer story to tell. They had had to let him go. His only compensation, which he had thought up and had enjoyed, had been to make the complaint against Sergeant Bergerac.

Carnegie and Tirrell were left with the certainty that the cocaine Dumoiter had been bringing them was somewhere on the Island, unless the thief had been a daytrip Frenchman who had taken it back to St Malo with him. That was unlikely. The gendarmes enjoyed harassing returning shoppers who liked to spend their money on this British outpost off their shore and made random thorough checks. Anyone bold enough to handle drugs that had come from France would not risk trying to take them back there.

Carnegie and Tirrell had their regular clients. The obvious thing to do was check whether any of these chose to give the next supply a miss. If any did, it would probably mean there was a fresh source on the Island, most likely at cut price. It would be the sure giveaway of the one-off seller, anxious to unload his stock fast.

None did refuse, however. All bought as usual. Sam Tirrell resigned himself to reporting to his boss that either the stolen consignment was being kept on ice for sale after they had ceased to look for it, or it had been flogged entire to someone rich enough to keep it for his own and his friends' use. Either way, it seemed they had lost it.

He was moving back towards the car when he felt a touch on the arm. Turning, he saw the skinny girl whose posh accent belied her constantly scruffy state. He thought she was going to spin him some hard luck story and ask if he would lend her her money back and let her pay next time. They often did, and he always refused. Cash for kind was the only way in this business involving unstable kids who might do anything if they got desperate enough.

But Stella was not asking: she was offering, and the offer she made caused Sam Tirrell, after a quick look round, to hurry her over to the car where Carnegie waited, and into the back seat with him beside her.

As he listened to her Bobby Carnegie was as quick as his

116

assistant to spot that they had struck lucky. He drove some way out of the town to where a disused gravel works lay back from the road. Then he switched off the engine and turned to smile at them in the back.

Stella was frightened. The peak of the euphoria had worn off and she had had to screw up her courage to make the approach. Their taking her away from the busy place to this one alarmed her, but she was committed now. She could only hope the man at the wheel had meant nothing more than what he had said in a friendly tone, that it would be safer to talk somewhere quieter.

'It's not very clever of this friend of yours to try to elbow his way in here, is it?' he asked now, with a concerned smile.

'He's not,' Stella insisted. 'He doesn't want to deal or anything. He just happens to have this stuff and he wants to sell it.'

'Well, that's wise of him. A businessman, d'you say? Anyone I know?'

'I . . . don't think so. I don't know his name myself.'

'Some friend,' commented Tirrell, who was not smiling. 'You know what, sunshine? If you and him are hoping to pull one on us, we won't be standing ready to look after you in future.'

'What I'm wondering,' Carnegie addressed Tirrell, 'is whether what he's trying to sell is ours already?'

He turned his smile on Stella again, raising an eyebrow.

'If so,' said Tirrell, 'the joker's wandering in a minefield.'

'It's genuine,' she insisted. 'He . . . wants to raise money without the tax people hearing. He's not trying to cut you out, or anything.'

Carnegie studied her thoughtfully. 'Well,' he said with calculated hesitancy, 'I'd like to help you, love – he has offered you a cut, I hope?'

She nodded.

'All right, then. You tell him I'll give him a fair price for what he's got – it he's really got it.'

The smile left his face abruptly. Stella stammered, 'Oh, he has. I'm sure he has.'

She felt her thin arm gripped suddenly by the man beside her. It hurt terribly. 'No monkey business, by either of you,' he warned.

'Go easy with the lady,' the man in front was saying. 'We don't want any nasty accidents, do we?'

Said with that smile, it was far more menacing than the open threat or the agonising grip, which was increased momentarily before it was released.

The driver started the car again and she was taken back to the area where they had picked her up.

'Make sure you pass on the message,' were Carnegie's parting words. 'Our friend here will be in touch to see what arrangements you've made.'

She nodded and got out. They watched her walk unsteadily away. Carnegie turned in his seat once more and jerked his head. The gesture ordered Sam Tirrell to follow her.

Chapter Sixteen

Tirrell watched her enter a telephone kiosk. He couldn't move close énough to try to overhear her; in any case, he saw, it wasn't necessary. Although she dialled three times she was getting no reply. She came out frowning, looking uncertain what to do. Then she made up her mind and set off at quite a brisk pace. He went after her.

It was all of a mile to Gloria Gibbins's villa at Grouville. Sam Tirrell was not much used to walking, but neither was Stella, and after the first few minutes he found it hard to hang back enough not to attract her notice.

He paused and watched where she turned in, then crept into the grounds after her. He found a poorly-kept, medium-sized villa in the pseudo-Spanish style, its paint flaking and weeds everywhere. Windows and doors were open, but there seemed to be no one about. He could hear the girl calling 'Simon?', 'Mrs Gibbins?' within the house. There was no answer, and eventually she came out, wandered round uncertainly, then set off droopingly back to town.

Tirrell didn't follow her at once this time. He went swiftly in, soon finding the note she had left asking Simon to look for her by the swimming pool. He used the telephone to. call Bobby Carnegie. Then he set off after her and soon had her in view.

The fact was that Gloria was making one of her increasingly rare efforts that afternoon. She had arranged a hair-do in town. She had been going to go by taxi, but Simon's unexpected arrival home had shown her the chance to save a pound. He had agreed to give her a lift, not expecting to hear from Stella so soon, and confident that she would ring again if she found him out. But after dropping his mother he had run into a couple of people who had leaned on the car roof and chatted to him at length through the window; and one of them, a girl, had coaxed him into a wine bar for coffee and a sandwich.

By the time that was finished, Simon was thinking he might as well drive by the swimming pool, just in case Stella happened to be there and had any news for him. She was there all right, sitting on the wall, resting her weary feet. Sam Tirrell, whose feet were equally tired, was perched on an iron railing behind her, watching.

He saw the orange Beetle pull up, but knew nothing of it or of the fair-haired kid who got out. When he saw him go to Stella, and the way she greeted him with obvious agitation, Tirrell got down off the rail and moved closer. Stella was glancing nervously about her, and suddenly she saw him. She gave a cry. The kid followed her look in Tirrell's direction and saw him coming fast towards them. Leaving the girl standing he raced towards his car. But Sam Tirrell was a professional. He reached the car before Simon could start it, yanked the door open, and shoved him across into the passenger seat. He leaped in, got the engine going, and roared away.

A few respectable holidaymakers noticed the brief incident and dismissed it as some crazy lark or the staged film happening that had become familiar on their television screens. The fact that no cameras were in evidence didn't trouble them. Telescopic lenses, and all that. They went on their way.

On the wall, the punks sat still, staring at nothing, their dim consciousness awash with the beating music. Stella looked about her, at a loss what to do. There seemed to be nothing. In one of the pockets of the man's jacket she wore there remained a little of the powder Simon had given her. She went down into the ladies' lavatory and used it. Then she drifted back up and subsided on to the wall with the rest of them.

Gloria asked the hairdresser to telephone her home to tell Simon she was nearly ready and would he mind picking her up again. There was no answer. She hailed a taxi. As soon as she stepped through her door she knew something was

120

wrong, and screamed. The taxi-man, just about to pull away, heard her and came to see what was wrong. The house had been ransacked by the men Bobby Carnegie had sent there by car after Sam Tirrell's phone call. The place was a shambles.

The taxi-man offered to call the police but Gloria said she would do it herself, asking him to wait meanwhile. She tried contacting Detective Sergeant Bergerac but was told he wasn't in. She refused to speak to anyone else. Instead, she asked the taxi-man to drive her over to Charlie Hungerford's.

Charlie was in one of his man-about-the-estate phases that afternoon, trimming off tree branches with a band saw. He looked curiously at the faded blonde woman approaching him from a taxi, and did a double-take as he recognised Gloria.

Coming so soon after Bergerac's reference to her, Charlie sensed something was up. Her hair was neat, he noticed, but her expensive dress was badly rumpled. He expected she was drunk. She didn't sound like it, though, and there was a genuinely pathetic air about the way she told him how her home had been done over and that she didn't know where to turn. His mind being the way it was, he half-expected an attempt at an insurance fiddle to try to raise money from the compensation.

'The police,' he suggested.

She shook her head violently. 'I can't. It's Simon.'

'Simon? Smashing his own home up? What'd he do that for?'

She shook her head again, and glanced at the taxi driver standing there uncertainly. Charlie went over and paid him and sent him away. He took Gloria by the arm and led her to a seat on the terrace overlooking the bay.

'Now then,' he said, 'what is it?'

'Your son-in-law – ex-, I mean – came to see me . . .'

'I know. He told me.'

'They've got him. I know they have.'

'Got who? Jim? What are we talking about?'

She seemed to have forgotten herself. She was staring about.

'You've got a lovely place here, Charlie.'

'Please, Gloria.'

'You used to come over to mine all the time.'

'Never mind that. What's happened? Gloria!'

She pulled herself together with an effort.

'Simon. He's got some drugs. He stole them and he's trying to sell them. Sergeant Bergerac came to warn me he was in danger . . .'

'Dear God!'

'I tried to phone him, but he's not there. Help me, Charlie. For old times' sake. Please.'

'Come on,' he said, and took her to the Rolls.

As they drove he used the car telephone to call the Bureau. Charlotte knew his voice at once. The last she had heard from Jim was that he was going to the vineyard to make himself presentable for his medical board. If he wasn't there, the Royal Barge was always worth a try, as his customary staging post. Charlie got no answer from the vineyard number. Diamanté Lil answered at the Barge. Jim had just looked in for a cup of coffee.

He was freshly shaved and in his best suit. He was feeling uncharacteristically nervous. At such a moment, at one time, a double brandy would have been his remedy – perhaps two or three. Coffee and some light banter with Lil were his chosen substitute.

There were no other customers at this afternoon hour. Charlie and Gloria told him the story in the bar, and she broke down.

'Give her a drink, Lil,' said Charlie.

'I've made such a mess of everything,' Gloria sobbed. 'It's all my fault. All of it.'

'Listen, Gloria,' Jim insisted, 'I need to know about this girl.'

'Her name's Stella.'

'Stella what?'

'It's all I know. I've never seen her. I don't know his friends.'

'No idea where I can find her?'

'There was a note she'd left for Simon by the telephone. Asked him to look for her by the swimming pool. It didn't say which.'

'I can guess,' Jim said, getting off his stool and glancing at his watch. 'Look after her, will you, Charlie?'

Hungerford nodded.

'Don't blame Simon,' Gloria pleaded. 'It's all my fault.'

'Never mind that. I'll do my best.'

Jim drove fast into town. A swimming pool, coupled with drugs in the case, meant one particular spot. He got out of the car at the open-air pool and approached the kids on the wall. The first two girls he questioned looked at him blankly and didn't answer, but a boy who overheard the name Stella pointed down the line towards a slight girl with a punk hairdo. She was huddled in her oversize man's jacket and Jim could see that she was shivering.

She looked frightened when he asked her where Simon was. He showed her his I/D card, and it reassured her.

'A guy took him in his car.'

'Simon's?'

'His Beetle, yes. He pushed him in and drove himself.'

'Know where to?'

So far as she was able, Stella had been thinking. She had remembered the quarry. It was in the direction the car had gone. She told him.

'This man,' he said. 'You know him?'

She shrugged.

'Come on!' he told her. 'He's probably taking your boy friend to pieces at this moment.'

The scared look returned.

'He's called Sam. He . . . comes round here.'

'A pusher?'

She nodded. Jim left her to it. She'd be easy enough to find later, when he'd need a statement. What might be happening now at the quarry was priority.

What was, in fact, happening there was that Sam Tirrell and the henchman who had been in the other car with Carnegie were standing over Simon, who had been dragged

123

into the hut where the departed quarrymen had taken their meals. The table and benches were still there, thick with stone dust and littered, like the floor, with abandoned tools and other junk.

Simon had been thrust on to one of the benches. Carnegie stood at the end of it, leaning on his stick. Sam Tirrell had Simon by the shirt front, bunching it tightly under his chin, forcing his head back. There were bruises on Simon's cheek bones and his nose was bleeding. The other man held his arms pinioned.

'You silly young bastard!' Carnegie said. 'We'll break your limbs one by one if you don't tell us where it is. You're playing a game out of your league. Now, talk.'

Simon kept silent. They had searched him thoroughly, gone all over the inside of his car and its engine compartment, but they hadn't found it. They wouldn't believe his denials that he had ever had the drugs and his insistence that Stella must have been stoned out of her mind and making the tale up. They knew he was lying; but if they were going to rough him up, he thought, he might as well come out of it with the drugs still his.

But they were right; they were not in the petty criminal class. Simon Gibbins had underestimated the ruthlessness of the drugs trade.

Tirrell drew back his free hand and smashed his fist into his face again. He hit him repeatedly, holding him so tightly with the other hand that he couldn't turn his head. The man holding his arms had his eye on an iron starting-handle lying amongst the rubbish. It would make a beautiful bone breaker.

'Hold on, Sam,' Carnegie ordered. Tirrell stopped hitting Simon, whose eyes were closed, blood streaking the lids from cuts above them. He slackened his grip on the shirt front momentarily. Simon's head lolled and his body sagged.

'You've put him out,' Carnegie said. 'No point wasting what he can't feel. Wait till he comes round again.'

'Where the hell's he got it?' Sam puffed from the effort. 'We can't go back to the bloody house. They'll have had the cops by now.'

'Try the car again.'

'We've been all through it.'

'Do it again. It was bound to be on him or in the car.'

They let Simon crumple to the floor. Carnegie stayed with him, searching every inch of his clothing yet again while the other two went out to the car, concentrating on the outside this time. Tirrell began removing the rear hub caps, the other man the front ones.

Jim saw the orange car and another one near it as he drove to the lip of the quarry. He backed off fast, so that neither of the men saw him. He turned into the road once used by the lorries to remove the gravel and drove down it at high speed. They didn't hear him coming, though; for inside the front nearside cap Sam Tirrell's companion had found the sachet of cocaine.

The man almost ran into the hut to receive his boss's congratulations. Tirrell, grinning hugely, was following when Jim's sports car zoomed up and squealed to a halt inches from him, stopping Tirrell in his tracks from the surprise. Jim leaped out and grabbed him. He shoved him through the hut's open door; and the starting handle, which the other man had grabbed on hearing the car, cracked down on Tirrell's skull.

'Thanks,' Jim grunted and went for the other man before he could raise the handle again. He was aware of another figure there, but one at a time would do. He grappled with his opponent and they fell across the bench and the table top squirming for advantage, giving Carnegie the chance to edge past.

Jim saw him out of the corner of his eye, though without recognising him. He banged the other man's head hard down on the table top and at the same time drove his knee viciously into his groin. The man shrieked and fell away, all resistance finished.

Simon lay motionless on the floor. Jim decided there would be time to attend to him later, after he had got the third man who had slipped out of the hut. He ran out and looked for him in the direction of the cars, but he had not gone that way. He was not in sight.

Jim guessed he was the boss, from the way it had been the

125

other two doing the work and the fighting. It was vital to catch him. The others would most likely not talk, and there was no certainty that Simon Gibbins would know him, in which case he might get off the Island unidentified.

A movement caught Jim's attention. He was facing the machine block of the gravel works, where an everlasting belt had carried the materials to the loading bay. He thought he had seen someone in the enclosed gantry where the belt's controls would be. He ran forward and vaulted on to the belt, intending to scramble up it. He heard machinery start up and it immediately began to move, taking up its slack with a jerk which tossed him up and aside, to fall on the ground.

The belt continued to rumble along. Jim picked himself up unhurt and ran into the building. A series of steep iron steps led up to the gantry. He took a deep breath and started up them.

A rain of gravel scattered about him. A glance upward showed the man up there scooping up old gravel from the belt in a bucket. Jim ducked his head as he saw the bucket swing and more gravel poured down. He kept on going, knowing it could not damage him.

The bucket itself came clattering down, bouncing on the steps but missing him completely. He risked another glance upward and found he was almost at the gantry. The man was standing, a silhouette against the light of the sky, bracing himself by his hands on a steel rail, a foot poised to smash down on Jim when he came within reach.

He took a deep breath, reached up his hands, and stumbled up the last steps as fast as he could go, clutching for the descending foot. He only half got it, and expected the other foot to crash down on his arms. It didn't. The man cursed and seemed to overbalance, falling to his knees. As Jim dragged himself up the last steps and stood on the gantry platform the man before him lunged at his ankles with a thick walking stick. Its hook went neatly round one of Jim's legs and a big heave pulled him over.

Falling almost face to face with the other man he recognised Bobby Carnegie. And in that same instant he saw a gold St Nicholas medallion dangling by a chain from his

126

thick neck. His mind flashed back to that agonising moment at the harbourside when his leg had been crushed between the boat and the wall; and simultaneously he remembered why he had thought he recognised this man.

Fortunately, the realisation didn't distract him. Carnegie was lunging for his throat and Jim's hands were holding him off.

'It was you, you bastard!' he gasped as each strove to break the other's grasp. 'You crushed my leg.'

'It's a pity . . . it wasn't . . . your bloody head,' Carnegie panted.

With a great effort he levered himself to his feet, tore his arms from Jim's hands, and tried to leap over him to escape by the metal ladder. But his own disability prevented him. He caught his leg, tripped, and fell on to the everlasting belt, which swooped him away towards the gravel chute.

'Stop the thing! Stop it!' he yelled. 'For Christ's sake . . .!'

Jim hadn't even time to get to his feet. With an awful cry Carnegie was swallowed by the chute's gaping mouth and disappeared. Jim struggled forward, to see him fall into the side of a pyramid of gravel down below. His impact caused an avalanche, and with a flailing of arms and legs and another scream he disappeared within seconds.

The gravel went on cascading and then was still. Jim knew there was nothing he could do. From the way he was shaking he knew he wouldn't have had the strength to try.

The nurse at the medical board room door stared at the dishevelled figure shambling down the corridor towards her.

'Bergerac,' it uttered. 'James Bergerac. I have a board.'

The nurse finished turning the key. 'You had,' she said. 'Over an hour ago.'

'Yes, I'm sorry, but . . .'

'The doctors managed to keep it. It's a pity you couldn't.' She looked him up and down.

'In any case, I very much doubt if they would have had you in, looking like that.'

127

She swept away and he could only stand there dumbly watching her.

When the long formalities attending the arrest and questioning of Tirrell and the other man, getting the badly beaten Simon Gibbins to hospital and the reclamation of Bobby Carnegie's body were over, and he had made his own preliminary report on the case, it was nearly nine. Jim would have dearly loved to collapse on to one of the Royal Barge's bar stools with an enormous scotch on the rocks.

Fortunately for his pledge, the mess he was in prevented his going there. He drove instead to the farm, where he knew there was nothing stronger than coffee.

His legs almost gave under him as he stepped out of the car, but an intriguing aroma issuing from the old building gave them the strength of curiosity. At his cooker, Francine turned to smile at him. She was wearing an evening gown.

'Perfect timing,' she said.

'What . . . are you doing?'

'*Boeuf en daube.*'

'I mean . . .'

'You said you would miss me. I decided I would miss you. There seemed only one answer to that.'

He went slowly to her, half-dazed by this last of the day's unrealities.

'I don't believe it!'

'Do you wish to?'

'Of . . . of course.'

They stood gazing at one another for long moments. Then she leaned forward and kissed him on the lips, fastidiously keeping her gown away from his filthy clothes.

'You need a wash,' she said. 'You may have a proper kiss afterwards.'

There were many, before and after the meal. During it, too. And with so many kisses within the cup, Jim never thought to ask for wine.

128

Chapter Seventeen

'Who are you? What are you doing?'

Jim straightened up from his scrutiny of the chart clipped to the metal foot of the hospital bed and faced the nun nursing sister who had come quietly into the intensive-care room. He had been hoping to find a name along with the medical particulars, but there was none.

He smiled apologetically at the frowning sister, who would be about his own age.

'I'm Detective Sergeant Bergerac, Bureau des Étrangers. You called us.'

'It doesn't entitle you to walk in here on your own. The man's critically ill.'

She was stating the obvious. The unconscious patient was wired up to two winking monitors and a saline drip was feeding a vein in his arm. So far as the bandaging on his head made it possible to judge, he too would be in his early thirties.

'Sorry,' Jim smiled again, seeking to appease her but not seeming to be succeeding. 'What happened?'

'He was found on the rocks at Gorey. A severe blow on the back of his head.'

'A fall?'

'The ambulance men didn't think so. There was a half empty can of beer beside him. They thought he'd been sitting there drinking it.'

Jim moved closer to look more closely at the pallid features.

'Don't touch him, please,' the sister ordered sharply. He stood back obediently.

'Do you know who he is?' he asked her.

'No.'

'Then why not the police? Why call the Bureau?'

'Because he's a visitor to the Island.'

'How d'you know that?'

From a side table she picked up a key attached to a heavy plastic tag. She handed it to him. He read on it PLEASE RETURN TO THE CASTLE HOTEL, GOREY, JERSEY.

'Islanders don't stay in their own hotels,' she said, and when he glanced up this time he saw a sardonic smile. 'This is all he had when he was found.'

'You missed your vocation, Sister.'

'Perhaps we should swop jobs – Jim.'

Her smile had a different quality now. She placed her hands flat against her forehead to hide the white wimple.

'Remember me now? We were at school together.'

'Nancy Villiers?'

'As was.'

'Good Lord! I mean, er . . .'

'Never mind.' They shook hands. Her expression changed to seriousness again. 'What will you do now?'

'See what the hotel can tell us. I'll let you know.' Instinctively lowering his voice he asked, 'What are his chances?'

'It's too early to tell. It must have been a savage blow. It will depend how long he stays like this.'

'Keep us informed. Nice to see you again, Nancy.'

He left and went out into the dusk, to get his car and drive to Gorey.

Gorey is the Island's easternmost tip, no more than fourteen miles from that department of north-western France called Manche. Normandy became part of France in 1205, but these islands so close offshore chose to stay loyal to the English Crown, so it seemed prudent to build a defensive castle on Gorey's rocky height, Mont Orgueil. The name translates as Mount Pride, an aptness which has grown since Jersey's tourism boom of recent decades. At night when the sheer granite faces of the fortress are bathed in silver-blue floodlighting, it reflects down on to the harbour water and its throng of small craft and makes an impressive spectacle.

The effect is heightened by the coloured lights of the

restaurants and hotels which line the harbour front, one of which, inevitably, is called The Castle. Its manager, new to Jim, led the way to the room whose door opened with the anonymous casualty's key. He saw the usual personal odds and ends of the temporary hotel guest. An unusual feature of this one was a portable typewriter on the dressing table with a blue box of blank paper beside it, some sheets of carbon and a packet of paper erasers.

'He's some kind of writer, I think,' the manager said. 'He goes out at eight every morning, comes back about six, has a couple of drinks, dinner, then comes up here and types for hours. There's been one or two complaints when he's gone on extra late.'

'Stanley Morton, you say he's called?' said Jim. The name rang no bells for him.

'That's right. Over from London. Australian or New Zealand from his accent, I'd say.'

'Could he be a travel writer, then?'

'Hardly likely. The Tourism people generally book them in and they're only short stayers. He's been here three weeks. We thought at first he might be one of the good food people. They like to do their own thing. But he always eats here, so that can't be it.'

Jim had been searching around, opening drawers and the wardrobe. Beyond clothes and effects he found nothing.

'Not much to show for all that typing,' he remarked.

'I tell you another thing, Sergeant – he doesn't leave any discards in the wastepaper basket.'

'You play cops, too, do you?' Jim grinned, remembering the shrewd nun, the former Nancy Villiers.

'You notice things instinctively in this business,' the manager shrugged. 'The wife came up one night there was a complaint and noticed the w.p.b. was full. We were a maid short next morning so she did his room herself, and there wasn't a scrap left in it. He must have taken it out and got rid of it himself.'

'Strange folks, writers, aren't they?'

'We decided he must carry his work in that briefcase of his.'

131

'Briefcase?'

'One of those red leather things you see advertised. He's never without it.'

He was when he was found, Jim thought; and knew this was going to be an investigation with a difference.

Stanley Morton had had the briefcase with him that morning when he had taken his usual early bus from Gorey to a small place on the coast a little under two miles away. He liked the bus ride; better than driving a hire car along the narrow lanes, constantly alert for someone coming from the opposite direction. Many of the roads were only one car's width, with passing places at intervals. Over-confident locals, expecting to have the roads to themselves so early in the day, were the morning menace to the stranger-driver; reckless or incompetent visitors were the danger on the way back to Gorey in the late afternoon.

The bus trip, right after bed and breakfast, was a pleasant buffer period before the day's concentration on work. Morton enjoyed staring out at the blue sea and rock-scapes, and inland to pastures where the long-lashed cows grazed, the sloping *cotils* where potatoes and outdoor tomatoes grew, the little patches of cultivated roadside garden, colourful with hydrangeas, and getting frequent glimpses of wildflowers in hedgerows and fields, a sight he had seldom seen in England where he had lived for the past several years.

He had been a feature writer with the *Sydney Sun's* Fleet Street bureau. His job brought him into contact with many interviewees, amongst them a number of men and women who had had stirring wartime experiences. In the case of one, a woman who had been in a Japanese prisoner of war camp in Singapore, he had recognised that there was enough material for a whole book and he had been commissioned by a paperback house to write it. He had bought a portable recorder and spent many hours in the woman's company, listening to her memories, encouraging her to give details which she might have passed over as irrelevant, but which he

132

knew would add vital colour and drama to the story.

'It's like the psychiatrist's couch,' she had told him, as he took her back through those traumatic times.

Back at his flat he played over the recordings and bashed his portable typewriter. What the narrative lacked he supplied himself, sometimes from read-up detail, often from his imagination. When he showed the result to the woman, she said she was sure he had got it absolutely right; fading memory would account for the unfamiliarity of some of the touches he had put in.

The publisher recognised a good, punchy tale, and the name of Stanley Morton made its first appearance on a book jacket depicting a half-naked European woman cowering from the bayonet of a snarling Japanese soldier.

By the time his London stint for his paper was up he had had two more books published and was well into another. His name was becoming known in publishing circles for this sort of writing. He resigned from the *Sydney Sun* to stay in London and freelance, both under his own name and as a ghost-writer when it made better marketing sense for the subject to seem to be telling his own story.

It was just such a ghosting assignment that had brought him to Jersey. A publisher named Voss had sent him to work with a retired army major who had a story to tell which Voss knew would be right up Morton's particular street. It had taken only one evening and a bottle of whisky with Major Gerald Furneaux to convince Morton that this was so. He had flown back to London, hired certain 16-millimetre films through one of the agencies, and taken them straight back to the Island.

In St Helier he hired a projector and took it to the modest coastal cottage where the Major lived in retirement with his wife. There the two men had settled down to day-long sessions of recording, using the films to prompt memories from thirty years previously; and each evening Stanley Morton had pounded out the story in his hotel, occasionally to the annoyance of occupants of neighbouring rooms.

This morning he had a new can of film with him, flown over the day before and delivered to the hotel.

'What, more!' exclaimed Major Furneaux, as he shook Morton's hand and ushered him in. The Major was in his early fifties, his hair already grizzled and his face testifying to heavy drinking. He was dressed in the retired regular officer's uniform of cavalry twill slacks, checked Viyella shirt with regimental tie, baggy green pullover and suede half-boots.

Morton grinned and went to thread the film through the projector.

'They say it was the most reported war in history,' he said. 'Chap I knew covered it for the *Sun*. He reckoned some of the Yank correspondents didn't go much closer than the bar of the Tokyo Press Club. There were plenty up the sharp end, though.'

'Can't say I remember 'em,' the Major said. 'Fighting men don't pay much attention to odds and sods.'

He drew the curtains to darken the littered room, his personal domain in the cottage. Photographs of military groups were on the walls. A couple of painted metal figures of soldiers were amongst the few ornaments, which were mostly of oriental origin. A drinks cabinet loomed large in a corner near the writing desk.

Morton ran the film once with its sound track, then again without sound. This time Major Furneaux supplied commentary and comments, which Morton recorded on his Japanese cassette machine.

'God-forsaken place,' the Major remarked of a panning shot along coastline utterly uninviting in contrast with the Island's. 'They say the Koreans encouraged erosion in old times so that if anyone came sailing by, looking for a spot of land to annex, they wouldn't give theirs a second glance.'

There was a sequence showing ruined Seoul, its broad thoroughfares empty of any people or traffic other than uniformed Americans and South Koreans.

'Hardly a pane of glass intact in the whole bloody place,' was the Major's comment. 'Few Gook civilians scratching about in the ruins. Damn all else.'

Then came more shots of the devastation wrought by that

134

to-and-fro war. The film had been made during the pro-tracted peace talks at Panmunjon, but there were some action sequences of Australians going out on patrol, New Zealand artillery firing, British infantry, Turks, Indians, Americans: a cross-section of the United Nations' forces.

'Worst sort of war,' the Major said, at the end. 'Most of our side without a clue what we were fighting for, or why it was worth it for a place like that. Then their lot coming from the north in screaming hordes, blowing bugles, not caring how many they lost because there were plenty more following, and our chaps stood and fought 'em off as if they were defending England herself. I remember one affair near Pyongyang – Hill 41 . . .'

He talked on, stimulated by the film, and while his recorder ran Stanley Morton jotted notes on a pad to remind him of questions to ask and thoughts for action passages he would make up and slot in. It was satisfying work, and well paid, with a share of spin-off possibilities beyond the book itself.

They had drinks before lunch, which was served in the kitchen-diner by Edith Furneaux, the Major's wife, a thin, worried-looking woman a little younger than he. Morton tried to jolly her along, but sensed she didn't care for him.

'I was saying to your husband there could be film interest,' he encouraged her. 'Lot of money in that.'

She made no comment. The Major said, 'The main thing is to get the thing published. The rest can follow.'

Morton left it at that. It was plain to him that they had little money. Their place was sparse and shabby. They had no car, only a shabby Land Rover, and he had never·seen either of them dressed differently from today. It was as well for the Major, in view of his capacity and need for strong drink, that whisky in the Island was half the mainland price.

The Korean War had been thirty years ago, yet only now had he decided to tell his part of it. It was obvious to Morton that the need to make money was the reason. Yet he sensed something more; something personal, detected from the man's tone when he mentioned certain fellow officers' names

135

and events. It had taken a week of getting to know and trust the writer before Gerald Furneaux had described the incident which could give his book sensation value and provide the hard core around which to spin the narrative. Then Morton had understood that money was only the incidental factor. This man had been biding his time until he could speak out freely.

When he had heard what he had to tell, Stanley Morton was glad that his contract as anonymous ghostwriter had a clause indemnifying him against any action arising from assertions made in the book. He told himself he would make sure of such a precaution in future work of this kind.

It never occurred to him, as he sat on the rocks that evening, enjoying a beer in the fresh air before going back to his hotel for dinner and a long evening's writing, that this contract would be his last.

Chapter Eighteen

The typewriter which had served Stanley Morton for years lay on a table in the general office of the Bureau des Étrangers. The platen and ribbon had been removed. Jim Bergerac was peering closely at the former, watched by a States Police laboratory assistant named Joe. Charlotte was at her desk, her arms folded on her typewriter top, watching and listening with interest.

'The user smokes and likes strawberry jam,' Joe pronounced, with a wink at her. 'He doesn't clean the typeface much, and he bangs the keys, probably a two-fingers-and-thumb sort.'

'A journalist,' Charlotte said. 'I once had a boyfriend on the *Jersey Evening Post*. They never bother learning to touch type.'

The telephone rang. She picked it up.

'Bureau des Étrangers. Good morning.' It was the day after the attack on Stanley Morton.

'This'll tell you more,' Joe said to Jim, picking up the ribbon and a watchmaker's lens. 'It's quite new. Only been typed over a couple or three times. It's possible to read the odd word.'

Jim screwed the lens into his eye. 'Where?'

Joe pointed to a place he had marked with a paper-clip. Jim brought it up to the lens.

' "Korea",' Joe prompted him. 'At the other places I've marked you can make out "attack" and "guns". There's also what might be a name. "Lieutenant F-u-r . . . something." I can't get any more of it.'

'Furneaux,' said Charlotte behind them. They turned to stare, Jim letting the lens drop from his eye into his cupped hand. She beamed at them as she replaced the receiver.

'How d'you know that?' Joe demanded.

'If you promise never to read my ribbons I might tell you.'

'Come on!' Jim ordered.

'That was the manager of Gorey Castle Hotel. He said he had a call from someone this morning asking if Stanley Morton had been delayed or something, because he'd been expecting him.'

'Who?'

She glanced at her pad. 'A Major Furneaux, Myong Cottage, Portelet Bay.'

'Well, well! What did he tell him?'

'He'd had an accident and was in hospital. He thought he'd better not say any more, with the enquiry in your hands.'

'Good. Myong Cottage, Portelet Bay. Give Major Furneaux a ring, love, please.'

While Charlotte looked up the number and dialled Jim scrutinised the ribbon at the points Joe indicated. She interrupted him.

'Major Furneaux isn't in. His wife thinks he'll be at the Yacht Club now.'

'Thanks. Tell her I'll try to find him there.'

He thanked Joe and left the Bureau. The St Helier Yacht Club was only a few minutes' walk away and Jim gave his restored leg the benefit of the exercise. He was waiting for another medical board to be arranged. He felt fully fit now and had no doubts that he would pass, especially with another result or two to override any doubts.

It was only just eleven, but he wasn't surprised to find a sprinkling of members in the pleasant clubhouse, talking at the bar and seated at tables with glasses in front of them. He was waiting to ask the steward to point out Major Furneaux for him, but the man was on the telephone. Spotting Charlie Hungerford sitting alone, wearing sailing gear, Jim went to join him.

'Hello, Jim,' he was greeted by. 'Who let you in here?' It was said with the usual smile, but the condescending implication was there.

'I'm looking for a Major Furneaux. Know him, Charlie?'

138

Charlie pointed to the full whisky glass across the table from his own.

'Back in a tick. Just gone to reception to collect a message or something. Sit down and have his glass. I paid for it.'

'You know I don't any more.'

'Ah, keep forgetting. Another man gone wrong.'

Jim sat in a spare chair, asking, 'Friend of yours, is he?'

'Fellow member. Great knack of getting called away just when it's his round that's being fetched.'

Jim looked round. There had been no one else waiting at the reception desk. He saw the door of the Gents open and a man in his fifties come out, carrying a packet. He wore an old tweed jacket over a green pullover and cavalry twill slacks and he had a regimental tie round his neck. He was heading their way, and there was no doubt who he could be.

Charlie Hungerford introduced them and Jim explained his errand, saying nothing more about Morton's state than that he had perhaps been mugged, an uncommon but not unknown crime even here. He had noticed the Major's concerned expression as he approached, and saw his mouth tighten at this news.

'I'm off down to the boat,' Charlie interrupted, getting up. 'He'll only cost you an orange juice,' was his parting remark to the Major as he left them. The Major gestured an invitation to Jim to have a drink, but he shook his head.

'What's Mr Morton doing in Jersey, Major?'

'He and I are working on a book.' The Major licked his lips after answering. He was clearly ill at ease.

'What sort of book, sir?'

'War story . . . Men under fire. That sort of thing.'

'Based on your experiences in Korea?' Jim hazarded, and got a surprised look.

'I . . . did my spell there, yes. He's writing this . . . this novel, and he wanted some background, he calls it. Got in touch with me, and I said I'd oblige.'

Jim left unasked the direct question of why an Australian novelist should come over from London to get background information from a retired officer in Jersey when there would have been any number of sources available to him over there. Perhaps Major Furneaux had distinguished himself in that war. He chose to leave that, too.

'He's been taking up quite a bit of your time, I understand?'

'Well, yes. I'm retired, you know.'

'I hope you're getting something out of it,' Jim smiled.

He got a nervous little twitch of a smile back.

'Yes, yes. Not grumbling.'

'We understand he carried a red leather briefcase with him wherever he went.'

'I . . . seem to recall it. One doesn't take much notice of such things.'

'So you'd have no idea what he kept in it, sir?'

The Major laughed artificially. 'Wouldn't be his lunch. We always give him that.'

'The last time was yesterday?'

'That's right. I'd asked him to come a bit later this morning. Nine-thirty, ten. I wanted to get out in the boat and catch a fish or two. Punctual chap. When he didn't show up I telephoned his hotel.'

'Major, when you and he talked, did he take notes?'

'Quite a bit.'

'In a notebook? A recorder?'

'Bit of both.'

'So he'd probably have had them with him in his briefcase when he left you yesterday at . . .?'

'About half-five, as usual. He always catches a bus.' He finished his drink and got up. 'Must be getting back, Sergeant. The wife will be wondering.'

'Only one more question, Major.' Jim had also risen. 'His notes, or anything he's written up from them – he hasn't left them at your house, by any chance?'

The Major shook his head firmly.

'He comes and asks me questions, and I answer those I can. Other than that I know nothing about Mr Morton or his working habits. Just glad to help a chap who cares to get his facts straight, that's all. Sorry I can't tell you more.'

140

He nodded and walked quickly away. Jim gazed after him, wondering why he appeared so on edge and had certainly been less than frank.

It occurred to him to walk along to the jetty where he knew Charlie Hungerford's yacht lay. He had been taken out in her often enough with Deborah and Kim, and sometimes by Charlie alone, in his son-in-law days.

Charlie was on deck. He had been draining and checking the fresh water tank and was preparing to refill it. He gestured Jim aboard.

'How are Deborah and Kim?' Jim asked. He knew that his growing interest in Francine had taken his mind off them. It wouldn't bother his ex-wife, but Kim would feel it if he neglected her.

'Kim's fine. Asking about you a bit.'

'I've been busy. One enquiry after another.'

'Deb's all right. She's got her own interests, you know.'

Jeremy, hadn't Kim told him the boyfriend's name was? He hadn't asked about him or tried to find anything out. Although they were split up now, and he and Francine had been sleeping together since that night she had decided to stay on, he felt the male's irrational jealousy of any man allowed to touch intimately a woman who had been his.

'How well d'you know Major Furneaux?' he asked as casually as he could.

Charlie went on working without looking up.

'Hardly at all. Good basis for friendship, that. No obligations. Been up to something, has he?'

'Writing a book.'

Charlie glanced up with a comic expression. 'Writing a what? He's quite good at I.O.U.s – plenty of practice with 'em – and notes explaining why he can't pay his club dues. I'd never pick him for an author. Not in this world.'

'We all have a secret life, Charlie. After all,' Jim couldn't resist it, 'where were you in the war, ex-father-in-law?'

'I did my bit.'

'Pay Corps, Aberystwyth, wasn't it?'

141

The millionaire bared his teeth. 'Two bloody years in North Africa.'

'Oh, yes. A lance-corporal, flogging army stuff to the Bedouins.'

'If you want to be offensive you can get the hell off my boat.' He added in a hurt tone, 'Anyway, it was surplus. Surplus to requirements.'

'Though not strictly yours to sell.'

'If I hadn't, someone else would. It's a pity they did away with National Service. A spell in the army would have done someone like you good.'

'It set you up all right, Charlie.'

Jim turned to step ashore.

'All right, I'm going. I just wondered if your Major friend's another one pretending to be something he isn't.'

Charlie shook the water hose nozzle at him.

'He went through the Korean War. Couple of years a prisoner. That's more than a feckless berk like you could have managed.'

'I wouldn't know. I don't think I was even born. So long, Charlie. Love to all.'

He swung ashore and strode away.

He went back to Royal Square, but this time he turned towards the tall solid block of a grey granite building which occupied the whole of one side. It had red painted doors, picked out in gilt, with colourful royal arms set above two of them. A wall tablet stated that one of the doors belonged to the Court House, rebuilt from the 1764-69 original. Another bore the sign BIBLIOTHÈQUE PUBLIQUE 1886.

'Stanley Morton,' the woman librarian at the desk answered his enquiry without needing to consult the catalogue. 'War books. People's experiences, you know. Rather lurid. Men read them.'

'Thank *you*,' Jim grinned. 'Can you tell me his publisher?'

That she did need to look up. Only one of Morton's books was on the shelf. Jim noted the publisher's name and address and turned to the back flap of the jacket. There was a thumbnail biography of the author, confirming that he was

142

an Australian and a former journalist, but adding nothing else of significance.

The girl looked up the publisher's telephone number for him in a book trade directory. She added, 'The boss man there's called Hedley Voss. He gets as much publicity as his authors.'

'Whizz-kid?'

'That's right. One of the transatlantic commuting brigade.'

'Thanks.'

'Do you want to borrow this book?'

He had flipped through some of its pages.

'I don't think it'll advance my education or improve my mind, do you?'

She shook her head, smiling, and he left, to walk the few paces across the paved Royal Square to his office, where Charlotte took only minutes to ascertain that Hedley Voss was in his London office, and, upon stating that it was Jersey States Police business, to persuade the secretary to put him on the line.

'Bureau des Étrangers!' echoed Voss, when Jim had introduced himself. 'Office of Strangers. How very Kafka!'

Jim, perched on the corner of Charlotte's desk, let the wry comment go.

'I'm calling about your author, Mr Stanley Morton.'

'Is he my author, Sergeant Bergerac?'

'You published a book of his that I've just been looking at.'

'The days of the one-publisher author are long departed.'

'So he isn't working for you at present?'

'Authors don't work for publishers. We enjoy temporary partnerships.'

Jim rolled his eyes at Charlotte, the flip evasiveness behind the public school accent irritating him.

'Then you've no interest in Mr Morton just now?'

'I don't think I quite said that.'

'Look, sir, I was calling to let you know that Mr Morton's met with an accident over here. He's in hospital, on the danger list. However, if the work he's over here to do doesn't concern you, we'll be grateful if you'll tell us whether there is an agent or anyone else we should contact.'

There was no immediate response. When Voss did speak again his tone was different.

'I apologise, Sergeant. The answer is, yes, I do have an interest in his present work.'

'The novel a Major Furneaux's helping him with?'

There was another pause before Voss answered, 'Yes.'

'There just could be a connection between the book and Mr Morton's accident. We wondered if you could throw any light on it for us.'

'Just possibly . . .'

'Then we'll be grateful if . . .'

'But not over the telephone. I'll come over there myself. The first available flight tomorrow.'

'I'll meet you at the airport, Mr Voss.'

'Thank you, Sergeant. I'll appreciate it.'

It sounded a different man who hung up.

At the very time Jim was having this telephone conversation, Major Furneaux was having one of his own. The difference, though, was that the Major had not initiated his, and he did not know the identity of the man who had called him at his cottage and was speaking to him in a smooth, hard tone.

'I hope you picked up our message at the Yacht Club, Major?'

'Who the hell are you?'

'That's immaterial, just so long as our message was received and understood.'

The Major's wife appeared unseen by him in the doorway of his room and listened fearfully as he replied.

'You understand this. You can destroy as many notes and tapes as you like, but you won't destroy my memory. I know what happened, and I'm determined other people should read about it. So, whoever you are, you can go to hell. That book is going to be finished, and published.'

Edith Furneaux was too far away, and the caller's voice

144

was too low-pitched, for her to hear his response.

'Sober up, Major. And watch out. You've been warned.'

The Major slammed his receiver down. He picked up the glass of whisky he had been drinking and drained it at a gulp. As he went for the bottle he saw his wife standing there.

'Gerald . . .' she began, moving towards him. He waved her away with a jerk of the bottle.

'Don't start again, Edith. You're getting boring.'

'It's you I'm concerned about, Gerald. I know we need the money, but I wish you'd give it up.'

'Nag, nag, nag!' he complained as he poured.

She flashed back, 'We wouldn't have so many debts if you'd drink less.'

He returned her a look of total disdain.

'When you understand what you're talking about, *my dear*, we can have an intelligent discussion.'

He raised the fresh glassful to his lips.

Chapter Nineteen

Voss's secretary called back later to say that he wouldn't be on the early flight after all but on the next one, arriving Jersey 11.55.

Jim had no trouble identifying him when he came out of the Arrivals channel into the long, narrow airport concourse and paused to look round expectantly. He was in his mid-thirties, slim and extremely well groomed in a hand-tailored lightweight suit, silk shirt, matching tie and handkerchief and Gucci shoes. Jim knew they were Gucci because he had a pair he kept for best, a relic of being married to a rich wife who gave him presents.

He introduced himself and showed his I/D card. They shook hands. Voss was watchful, with dark, intelligent eyes.

'Any luggage, sir?' Jim asked.

'Only this.' Voss held up a leather briefcase of the type with space for a change of clothes in addition to the documents. 'I hope I might get back tonight, anyway.'

'The last flight's 20.00.'

'See how we go.'

'The car's this way, Mr Voss.'

They went out, taking no notice of two other men who were greeting one another. Both were in their twenties, more casually dressed than Voss but neat and well set-up physically, as though they might be policemen or soldiers in civvies.

'Good flight, Cropley?' asked Kinthly, the one who had been waiting for the other's arrival.

'Thank you, sir.' Cropley was the heavier built of the two. Kinthly looked him over approvingly.

'Still boxing?'

'And climbing, sir. Bit of everything.'

'Good man.'

Cropley picked up the well-travelled hold-all that was all his luggage and followed Kinthly to the car park. They glanced admiringly at the well-kept old Triumph Roadster which was pulling out. Beyond that there was no recognition. The two pairs of men had never met.

In the Triumph Voss asked, 'What's the latest on Stanley Morton?'

'No change, I'm afraid. Unconscious in intensive care. I rang them just before I came out here.'

'Too bad. Useful hack. Always willing and delivers on time, which is more than one can say for most of them.'

Jim noted the emphasis was on business rather than compassion.

'No point in going to see him, then,' Voss went on.

'Not really. You'll want to look up Major Furneaux, though?'

'Yes. I've got quite a few thousand invested in him. Is his place on our way now?'

Jim automatically glanced at his watch. 'At this time of day he's more likely to be at the Yacht Club.'

'You don't surprise me,' Voss said. 'I hope Stanley's been keeping the old lush up to scratch.'

'You know him well, then?'

'Only met him once, to talk the deal over. At lunch. I noticed how eager he was for his refills. Speaking of lunch, I don't intend passing up a chance to have a go at your famous seafood. Join me?'

'If we go Dutch.'

Voss laughed. ' "No thanks, sir, I won't accept a drink on duty," ' eh? See how we get on, shall we?'

Jim returned him a grin. 'I know one of the best spots in the Island. It's called the Royal Barge.'

He headed the car towards St Aubin.

In the other car, a hired one, lunch was also mentioned.

'We're going straight into St Helier,' explained Kinthly, who was driving. 'Crab sandwiches and a beer.'

'Suits me, sir.'

'Fresh this morning. Their beer's good, too. Then I'll show you where to hire a motor bike.'

They, too, drove on their way. But while Bergerac and Voss kept their conversation deliberately general, reserving the business for over the table, Kinthly and Cropley kept to their purpose. They had a lot to arrange, and to make sure they got it right.

Although Hedley Voss was not a type Jim could imagine himself liking much, he was interested in this first encounter with a whizz-kid publishing type, a mixture of brash self-confidence and energy, no doubt fuelled by immense ambition. Having been introduced to Diamanté Lil, Voss took over the ordering of a luncheon far more lavish than Jim was accustomed to. If, at the end of it, he still felt he couldn't accept the other's hospitality without compromising himself, he would have to do some hard explaining back at the Bureau to justify his half-share of the bill.

When they had moved to their table and Gulliver's unsurpassed *Coquilles St Jacques* were before them, Voss began talking seriously without needing to be questioned.

'To begin with, Sergeant Bergerac, the book Stanley Morton's writing isn't a novel. Well, knowing Stanley, a good part of it will be fiction, but the guts of it is fact. And Furneaux isn't helping him. It's the other way round. I don't have to tell you what a ghost is, in the writing business?'

'No. I gather Morton has quite a line in it.'

'That's right. Furneaux came to me through a mutual acquaintance he'd asked for advice about how to approach getting a book published. I invited him to lunch and he told me the story. I knew at once it would be a seller, but I could see Furneaux would never manage to write it by himself. He knew it, too, and he was only too glad to be put in touch with Stanley.'

'They share the proceeds, presumably?'

'That's it, though Furneaux gets the greater cut and it's published under his name. If, by any chance, Stanley can't go on, I can easily put in another ghost to take over. If it had been Furneaux who'd been put out of action it would be a different matter. It's his story and my money that I'm concerned about.'

'Could someone else be?'

'They are.'

'Does Morton know?'

'Yes. I warned him not to leave his notes lying about where they might be got at. Is his hotel room secure while he's in hospital?'

'It's locked. But his notes aren't there and they're not at Furneaux's. I think he was carrying them in a briefcase he took everywhere. There's no trace of it.'

'Blast! It could mean starting from scratch again.'

It seemed that the loss of the notes wasn't of great significance in itself. Jim couldn't imagine publishing rivalry extending to knocking anyone over the head for a story which wasn't even his. The answer had to be in its contents.

'That's right,' Voss agreed. 'Even I wouldn't stoop to pinching someone else's idea by violence. We have much simpler methods. By God, this is a superb wine. Will it be cruel to make you watch me drink another bottle?'

'Not half as bad as if I weakened and shared it.'

'All right, gentlemen?' asked Lil, coming to take away the empty scallops herself.

'Superb,' said Voss. 'Another one of these, if you please.'

'Don't lead Jim astray, will you?'

'I don't think he's the easily-led type.'

They let their conversation lapse into generalities while Lil placed before them oval platters piled high with a quantity and variety of fresh seafood that made Voss's eyes pop.

'I can see I'll be coming back,' he said.

'*Bon appétit*,' Lil wished them, putting down the fresh bottle of wine and leaving them to go to work with the set of instruments for cracking, probing and extracting.

'Any suggestion why Morton was attacked, then?' Jim resumed.

'A frightener. To Furneaux.'

'Bit hard on Morton.'

'I agree. My guess is they conked him a bit harder than they'd intended, if indeed they'd intended to at all. You're the policeman, but I think you'll find they'd got a look into his hotel room at some stage and found he didn't keep his notes there, so they guessed at the briefcase. Their hope would be that Furneaux would take the hint and decide it would be too much bother to start all over again. If so, they reckoned without me. I don't chuck several thousand quid away for no end result.'

'Two obvious questions, then,' said Jim, working on a lobster claw. 'Who are "they"? And what's in the book that makes them go to these lengths to try to stop it?'

'First answer, I don't know. Second, do I have to? I don't want my book prejudiced by the Press spilling the beans about it.'

'If it's material to the crime, and we catch the criminal, it will come out. Major Furneaux and probably yourself would have to give evidence.'

'Oh, Christ!'

'But we haven't caught the criminal. We haven't found the briefcase. Morton may have left it on a bus, for all we know, and whoever hit him may have been the sort of punk who'll go for you if you so much as catch their eye. We'll know more when Morton comes round. Meanwhile, what you tell me stays off the record.'

Voss gave Jim a hard look and received a steady one back. He shrugged.

'It goes back to the Korean War, early fifties. Furneaux was a lieutenant in an infantry regiment. He went out in a scouting party commanded by a captain I'm going to call X. There was a reason to believe there were North Korean snipers hidden in a village. The few remaining inhabitants, mainly old folks and children, denied any knowledge. X refused to believe them. The boss man of the place stood on his dignity and said he wasn't having his people called liars. X ordered his soldiers to shoot him. They refused, so X grabbed an automatic weapon and did it himself. He went

150

berserk. He killed the lot, including a young woman with a kid in her arms.'

Jim asked, 'Who was Captain X, Mr Voss?'

Voss shook his head. 'I'm not telling until I have to in a court. As it is, I'm going to have to get someone to finish that book and drag publication forward, in case there is a trial and the story comes out. Come to think of it, if the timing's right my publicity people could make a meal out of it.'

He grinned suddenly, and Jim had a glimpse of the ruthlessness which, together with the disarming charm, accounted for this man's success.

Jim said, 'It was thirty years ago. Why wait till now?'

'Because X is now dead.'

'And you can't be sued for libelling the dead?'

'You've got it in one, Sergeant.'

'But the dead man's friends can try to stop you telling the story.'

'You're pretty warm. What does surprise me is that they should try.'

'Why is that, sir?'

'Because it isn't quite in the British Army tradition, so far as I understand it. I know the Colonel came over here to see Furneaux and try to beg him off.'

'Colonel?'

'Of the regiment. Furneaux asked my opinion and I told him he isn't under orders any more. He can do what he damn well likes. But, as I say, I can't see them resorting to banging people over the head.'

'So who would?' Jim gave up the unequal struggle with the amount of food and sat back. 'And what makes Furneaux so bitter against this dead man that he's determined to publish his story?'

'Because shortly after the patrol had left the village they were ambushed by North Korean soldiers. The bold Captain X made a dash for it and got away while the rest of them were fighting back. He was the only one not taken prisoner.'

Jim recalled his recent exchange with Charlie Hungerford.

151

'Someone told me Major Furneaux spent two years in a prison camp.'

'They were right. But only he and two men were still alive to be captured, and he later found out that the men had died as prisoners. Furneaux lived, as they say, to tell the tale and trade his memories for booze.'

Voss drank the last of his own wine. 'Bit like a paperback thriller plot, you're thinking? Embittered, hard-up ex-POW wants his own back on the coward who got away unscathed. It's a touch punchier than that, though. When Furneaux was released he found that the gallant Captain X had got himself hailed a war hero for reputedly shooting his way out of that ambush singlehanded. He'd been decorated, promoted. A few years later he left the army and became an MP. He got a lot of his votes for speaking out in the defence of the British soldiery alleged to have been beastly to the Mau Mau. Champion of the Poor Bloody Infantry, so to speak. He got a knighthood and . . . But I think I've given you enough of the picture, Sergeant.'

Voss turned, seeking Diamanté Lil's eye. When he caught it he put his fingers to his mouth to mime drinking from a coffee cup. She grinned and came to clear the things away.

'Poor old Stanley,' Voss said to Jim. 'But for him getting slugged on the head like that I'd never have eaten the best seafood of my life.'

Jim remembered that remark later, when the message came that Stanley Morton had died without regaining consciousness.

Chapter Twenty

Kinthly's right fist smashed into Cropley's face. It didn't break his nose, but brought blood pouring from it. Cropley's head had been driven back by the blow, but he went on standing to attention, as he had under the earlier facial blows which had cut open his cheek, and the ones to the body, meant to bruise.

'Good man,' said Kinthly, who was breathing heavily. 'That'll do.'

He took Cropley by the arm and led him across to where the Land Rover stood in the narrow country road just outside St Helier. He made him lean forward so that the stream from his nose was directed on to the offside headlamp and wing of the old vehicle. The glass of the lamp was already smashed and the wing buckled and shorn of some paint. Flakes of that paint were on the hired motor bike which lay under the hedgerow beside the vehicle. Kinthly pulled Cropley across to it as well and made sure that some more blood dripped on to it. He thrust the man down to smear some of it on to his clothes.

'Right,' he said. 'Well done. The rest's up to you. You won't have to wait long before someone comes along. Just hope it's a Good Samaritan.'

He grinned. Cropley noted the intense gleam in his eyes. They shook hands quickly, then Kinthly went to the Land Rover and drove off fast.

'Mad bastard!' Cropley swore aloud after him. His face and ribs hurt, as they did when he'd been through a half-dozen rounds in the ring. But he made no effort to staunch the nosebleed. Instead, he went to the motor bike and pulled it forward, so that it fell on to its side at the edge of the road. Its rear wheel was buckled from the impact when Kinthly had driven the Land Rover hard into it.

Cropley let some more blood drip on to it and the road around. Then he measured his distance and took a flying leap to a spot where he might have been flung had he been riding the bike when it was hit. It hurt when he landed on his bruised ribs and grazed his deliberately outflung hands. He cursed Kinthly again, and meant it; but as he waited for the sound of any vehicle approaching, hoping the driver would spot him in time to stop, he thought of the cheque he'd remitted to his London bank account from St Helier shortly after they'd finished those fresh crab sandwiches and that good beer, and it seemed a fair deal.

It wasn't long before a car came. The driver was a woman, careful of the bends in the narrow road. She stopped and went to the injured man's help. He was sitting up, holding his head in his hands, his crash helmet by his side. To her enquiry he answered that it had been a Land Rover that had hit him, coming up fast behind and mowing him down.

The driver had pulled up and come to him. He'd been drinking. That much he'd been able to notice from the chap's voice and breath as he'd leaned over him, and the way he'd walked. He'd seen the motorcyclist wasn't badly injured and offered him money for his trouble if he'd say nothing about it. When the offer was refused he'd sworn at him and gone back to the Land Rover and driven off. But he'd got its number.

The woman motorist was an Islander and conscious of the fact that it is an offence there to drive away from an accident or move any vehicle concerned in it without police consent. She stayed with Cropley until another car came. When one did she asked its driver to call the police from a box she knew was less than a quarter of a mile further on.

It took little time for a police car and an ambulance to get there. The police driver radioed in that the victim was a visitor to the Island and passed on the registration number he claimed to have seen. A search was put on the computer and within minutes the Land Rover's ownership had been traced to one G. Furneaux, Myong Cottage, Portelet Bay.

Quickly and efficiently though it was all done, it had left Kinthly plenty of time to complete his part of the operation.

He had driven the Land Rover back to Myong Cottage. He and Cropley had earlier followed it there on the motor bike from the Yacht Club, where they had waited a long time that evening for Major Furneaux to emerge. As Kinthly had noted on earlier evenings when he had kept this watch, the Major had been in scarcely a fit state to drive. They had followed him home, waited till he had gone in, then Kinthly had quietly driven off his Land Rover. The Major had even left the key in the ignition, saving him having to fiddle with the wires.

They drove back to their chosen spot, Kinthly smashed the Land Rover into the bike, then belted Cropley, who had stood and taken it, as he was being paid to do. Then Kinthly drove the Land Rover back to Myong Cottage, parked it undetected, and set off on foot back to his top-grade hotel in St Helier by a different route, not caring how long it took him and enjoying the quiet of the night and the sea-tangy air as he marched on his way.

The doctor in casualty who examined Cropley told him he could find nothing broken but thought it would be best to keep him overnight. Cropley thanked him pathetically and said what a kind lot they were in the Island. He was sure the bloke who'd run him down didn't belong there. Not the type.

The police soon knew differently and passed the details to the Bureau des Étrangers. Inspector Barney Crozier judged the matter serious enough to take charge himself. An extra factor was the victim's revelation that, in the ambulance, he'd chanced to find twenty pounds in Jersey currency stuffed in the breast pocket of his jacket. It certainly hadn't been there before the accident, he told them. He never kept money in such a place. The inference was obvious to Crozier.

So was the finding of blood and damage marks on the Land Rover standing outside Myong Cottage, its engine still warm. So, too, was the obviousness, when they rang the bell and were admitted by Edith Furneaux, that the man in the sitting room behind her, slumped in a chair, with a whisky bottle and glass on the table beside him, was far gone indeed.

'Dunno what you're on about,' was all he could keep

repeating in slurred response to Crozier's questions. They took him in, together with his Land Rover for tests.

Jim Bergerac was startled when he went into the Bureau next morning and was told by Charlotte that Major Furneaux was in custody, and in what circumstances. He had been woken in the night to take the telephone message that Stanley Morton was dead.

The news of the Major's being suspected of a hit-and-run alerted Jim. It was feasible that the heavy-drinking Furneaux had had a few more than usual last night. Voss may well have been leaning on him to get the book finished in double-quick time.

The publisher had declined Jim's offer to take him from the Royal Barge to Furneaux's place. He had preferred a cab. Jim had taken the hint that he had been told enough, and the rest would be private business. Morton's death changed that, though. He dialled the number of Voss's firm.

'Did Mr Voss get back from Jersey last night?' he asked the secretary.

'He came this morning. There's a very early flight.'

'Is he in the office yet?'

'He is but . . .'

Jim told her firmly that she must interrupt the editorial meeting and bring him to the phone. She sounded apprehensive, but said she would see what she could do. He stayed on the line, rather than leave them to call back. Within a minute Voss spoke to him.

'Hello, Sergeant. Excellent day, that was. I decided there was no point rushing back when British Airways do a 7.45 a.m. flight, so I treated myself to another seafood nosh-up. Place I was recommended to at St Brelade's Bay. You must know it. The . . .'

'Mr Voss, Morton died in the night.'

The other end of the line went silent. Then there came a quiet, 'Poor old Stanley.'

'It puts a different complexion on the enquiry. It could be

156

murder. I'm sorry, but certain things you told me yesterday can no longer stay off the record.'

'Of course. I appreciate that.'

'I'd like to know what regiment Major Furneaux served with, and the name of Captain X.'

He heard Voss sigh; but he got his answers. He also learned that the regimental headquarters was in London.

'Has Major Furneaux told you of any threats or warnings made to him directly?' he asked.

'Only the Colonel's request not to publish. A pretty strong one, too, but no threats.'

'Did you tell Major Furneaux that Morton may have been attacked because of his book?'

'No. You asked me not to. I told him I'm putting publication forward, though, and I'd expect his co-operation in getting it finished smartly.'

'How did he react?'

'He's only too keen to get on. It was obvious to me his wife wants him to drop it, but they've spent half the advance and there's no way he could pay me back. I'll get someone to take Stanley's place. It'll take a few days to arrange, though.'

'Just as well, maybe. Major Furneaux had a bit of a car accident last night. He's not injured, but he might not be up to concentrating on work for the moment.'

'One bloody thing after another,' was Voss's final comment. 'Glad I got that extra meal for my pains.'

Barney Crozier refused to let Jim question the Major.

'I went out there myself. Saw the damage to his vehicle, the blood on it, engine still warm. He was stoned.'

'How about this morning?'

'He's half sober. I wouldn't put it any higher. Denies the whole thing, of course.'

'Can I read the other chap's statement?'

'Nothing to it. Biking along, suddenly sent flying. Chap driving the Land Rover could hardly walk. Tried to buy him off. Drove away when he wouldn't play. He got the registration number and found twenty quid stuffed in his pocket afterwards.'

'Has he identified Furneaux?'

'Straight off.'

'Wasn't all this in the dark?'

'His bike's headlamp was on him when he leaned over him.'

'What's Furneaux's story?'

'Yacht Club all evening. Drove home as usual. Sitting having his nightcap when we got there.'

'How did he react?'

'Didn't know what we were talking about. Hadn't even passed a motor bike all the way home, let alone hit one. Wouldn't have dreamed of not reporting an accident. The usual stuff. It's no use, Jim. This one's open and shut.'

'It may not be, Barney.'

'I haven't got your kind of sympathy for drunks,' Crozier retorted, his patience giving out. 'Especially ones who drive.' He went away into his office.

Jim said to Charlotte, 'This chap in the accident . . .'

'Edward John Cropley. From London.'

'On holiday?'

'Had a row with his wife. Wanted to get away for a few days to sort himself out — somewhere her brother wouldn't find him, I got the impression.'

'Where's he staying?'

'He isn't. He's going home. Said his near-brush with death had made him see things in perspective at last. I expect he'll be sobbing on her pillow tonight.'

'A philosopher, eh?'

'Looked more like a boxer to me. Or a soldier.'

'We've kept a good description, I suppose.'

'I saw him, if that's what you mean.'

Jim gave her his grin.

'Keep remembering him, will you? It might just come in handy.'

'What is it, Jim? He'll have to come back for the hearing.'

'I think there might be a bit more to all this. Something that can't wait that long.'

'Something big?'

158

'Could be, seeing our friend the Major's involved.'

'In that case, why not take a look at Mr Cropley yourself.'

'Where?'

'The airport. He's going home on the afternoon flight. If you hang about you'll hardly miss him. Late twenties, big, broad-shouldered, short-cut hair – and probably the only returning holidaymaker from Jersey with plaster on his face and an arm strapped up. I bet he'll boast to his pals he's been off somewhere skiing.'

'You're a useful girl, you know,' Jim told her.

'Nice to be appreciated. I hear I've lost my chances, though.'

'How d'you mean?'

'The girl from Tourism – the one Tom Draycott was dating regularly.'

'You don't miss much, do you?'

'Never know when it might come in useful. Good luck, Jim – on both counts.'

He leaned over to peck her cheek, then left. He had just decided he would do more than wait at the airport for a glimpse of Cropley. He would be on the same plane.

Because British Airways' flights between London and Jersey are little more than aerial bus journeys there are few formalities beyond booking a ticket and getting aboard. Seats are not reservable in advance. You state your preference for the smoking or non-smoking section when you check in and are allocated a seat. If you are a seasoned commuter you ask for your favourite seat number.

It suited Jim well. He got there far too early, so that he could have had any seat he wished; but instead of going to check-in he waited in his car, close to the place where the taxis and hotel cars drop their departing passengers. It wasn't until he saw the unmistakable Cropley that he got out of the Triumph.

Cropley wasn't alone. A second man, about his age, got out of the taxi with him, gesturing to its driver to wait. As the

159

car pulled aside to park this man picked up a worn hold-all and carried it into the terminal. Jim strode quickly after them, noting some similarity in their physique, although the other man was not of Cropley's bulk.

He got behind them in the check-in line. They said nothing he could hear, but he had the impression from Cropley's manner and nods that the other was in some way his superior and was giving some instructions.

Jim managed to note the seat allocated to Cropley and, as soon as he had moved away, requested one in the row behind it.

The other man was not travelling. He put down the hold-all in order to shake the hand of Cropley's uninjured arm. Jim noted that Cropley almost stiffened to attention, before picking up the hold-all and marching off briskly to the baggage security check and personal scan. Jim paused before following him, to get a good look at the other man who walked away back to his taxi.

Jim caught up behind Cropley through the search and body scan. Nothing suspicious showed up. Jim himself was carrying only a shoulder bag with clothing in it. He was able to stay close to Cropley, and keep there until the time came to board. He made no attempt to get into conversation.

Cropley bought a newspaper and read it throughout the flight. Jim looked out of the window, almost from the moment of take-off to that of touchdown.

It was his first flight since returning to the Island. Accelerating past the point where Tom Draycott had burned brought its sharp memory. An area of ground was still scorched. As they rose and turned above the green land he thought of Francine down there, shepherding her tourists somewhere, or, for all he knew, working on a portrait in someone's house or at the vineyard.

They had agreed from their first night together that they must remain their own persons. With the shambles of his marriage so close a shadow over his memory, and tragedy still a searing scar on Francine's, however much she might claim to have got over it, each knew that they must resist

160

starting to depend on the other – at least, for the time being.

They had come together physically almost inevitably. The free and easy proximity under the same roof, the sexual attraction each had felt almost immediately for the other, the need each had for someone to cling to and help blot out memory with togetherness of the senses: without realising it, they were doing these for one another, undemandingly and unselfishly, and in doing so were healing themselves as well.

Where it might lead they hadn't even discussed. Both knew instinctively that too much searching and rationalising might kill it altogether, whatever it was. Also, their relationship stood on less than firm ground. Francine was living barely within the Island's residential rules. Jim's almost miraculous run of professional fortune since his return still did not guarantee him a permanent place in the Force, and losing it would almost certainly mean having to leave Jersey, where he couldn't envisage finding any remotely similar work.

So they lived for the day, and the night, and saw each other when both were free, and made no demands. He hadn't even tried to get in touch with her to say he was off to the mainland. He could go and come back, and she might never know. It was a feeling of freedom he found himself relishing after the years under the dictatorship of Deborah and her money, which she had taken for granted made him her bondsman.

Charlie Hungerford knew the score, Jim was aware. The old rogue had taken malicious delight in observing his frustration. Charlie had been through the mill himself. As a young man he had married a girl from his own Yorkshire background. As a millionaire, he had found himself stuck with her, a hopeless misfit in the circles he had won entry to. He had given her every reason to divorce him, and would have sent her away a wealthy woman; but ineradicable insecurity had kept her clinging on, their quarrels souring their lives and doing a lot towards making Deborah the bitch Jim had too late discovered her to be.

Charlie Hungerford had been set free by his wife's slipping away into the ultimate security, death. Until his divorce, Jim

161

had been seeking freedom for himself through the anaesthetic properties of drink. But for his accident, which might have left him crippled for life, he knew he might have ruined himself by going on that way. Fate had worked it out for all of them.

Life mattered again to Jim Bergerac. He had started looking outward and forward again, instead of hopelessly within. Where Francine might fit into his future – and Kim, for that matter, if her mother didn't succeed in turning her into a copy of herself and alienating her from him – he wasn't ready to ponder.

What mattered for now was that the No Smoking and Fasten Seat Belts sign had lit up and they were sinking down the afternoon sky towards Heathrow. And that thought of Charlie Hungerford had reminded him of Major Furneaux, and again of the burly man who was clipping his belt in the seat in front of him.

Chapter Twenty-One

To Jim's relief, Cropley didn't make for the cab rank at Heathrow. The uniform London taxis are hard to follow and keep in view, especially when traffic is heavy on the motorway, as it certainly would be at this time of day.

He walked straight through the 'Nothing to declare' Customs channel and headed towards the Underground. It gave Jim no problem about keeping close to him and he had no hesitation about occupying the same carriage. Cropley got to his feet to alight at Barons Court. Jim followed.

Some five minutes' walk from the station Cropley turned into a side street. Jim hung back a little now, but saw him go into some premises about halfway along. He crossed to the other side of the road and sauntered past. A garage beside one of the bleak-fronted Victorian terraced houses had been converted into a car-spraying plant, with Cropley's name painted on its door.

As Jim passed, Cropley came out of the workshop, calling back to a mechanic there, and let himself into the house adjoining, closing the door after him.

Jim retraced his steps to the main road to look for a telephone box. He found one almost at once, neither vandalised nor out of order. He looked up the number of the regimental headquarters in one of the tattered directories and called it.

It took a long go-stop-go taxi to get to the old barracks in North London. The young Adjutant came to the lobby to receive him. He was wearing Number One uniform.

'We've a mess do this evening,' he explained. 'Due to start in half-an-hour.'

'I'm sorry. Took longer than I'd expected. If the Colonel could spare me just a few minutes, I'd be grateful.'

163

'D'you mind the bar? Time to give you a drink.'

'Just a squash or something, thanks.'

'Nothing in it?'

'No thanks. A quiet corner, if possible.'

He was taken into the bar where a dozen or so officers were drinking and talking loudly. The Colonel, a hard-jawed no-nonsense looking man in his forties, came from amongst them to shake Jim's hand, while the Adjutant fetched him an orange juice. They moved to a corner away from the others.

'Don't go, Julian,' the Colonel said to the Adjutant. 'I believe this is to do with Major Furneaux, Sergeant?'

'A book he's writing, sir.'

'Oh, that. Sheer muck-raking. One has to be charitable as far as possible. He was a POW for two years, and it didn't do him any good. He's a pretty heavy drinker, I gather, and not well-heeled. But that doesn't give him licence to set out to smear a deceased officer's good name and embarrass his family.'

'Sir John Kinthly, sir?'

'The late Colonel Sir John Kinthly, MC, MP. As different a type from Major Furneaux as you could get.'

'Do you know the substance of the book, sir?'

'I do. And if you're asking my opinion, it's a pack of lies, worked up to make some cash. I'll never cease to wonder at our libel laws. Once a man's dead you can say what you like about him in public without any fear of comeback, never mind how it affects his family – or his old regiment, for that matter.'

'I understand you made a personal attempt to persuade him not to go ahead.'

The Colonel shrugged. 'Unofficially. There was nothing I could do save appeal to his sense of honour. I could see I was wasting my time. But tell me, Sergeant, what brings your people into it?'

'A professional writer named Morton, who'd been hired to work with Major Furneaux, appears to have been the victim of an attack. He suffered severe head injuries. He died early this morning.'

'Someone gets attacked every few minutes nowadays, don't they?'

164

'Not in Jersey. There are reasons for believing it might have been meant as a warning-off to Major Furneaux that went too far.'

The Colonel gave Jim a beady look.

'I hope you're not here to ask if I had any hand in it.'

'Not at all, sir. All I came to find out was whether there is any basis of truth to Major Furneaux's story. All the dead man's notes seem to have disappeared. They might crop up anywhere – in print, even.'

'Well, I hope you find them, in that case. Find them and preferably destroy them. The Korean War records of the Regiment are quite clear. Colonel Kinthly – Captain, as he was then – made a courageous escape from an ambush against overwhelming odds by fighting his way out, when all his other people had been killed or let themselves be taken prisoner. That includes Furneaux. I don't mind adding for your ears that from all I've heard of him he was a remarkably gutless officer. He was never more than Acting Major, and only for a few weeks at that. If he'd any decency he wouldn't use the rank in civilian life.'

A white-coated mess waiter was hovering with a silver tray, on which were a bottle of red wine and a glass. The Adjutant was about to wave him away, but the Colonel beckoned him forward. The waiter poured a small measure of the wine into the glass. The Colonel took it, swirled it around the bowl, put it to his nose and then sipped a little. He nodded approval and returned the glass to the tray. The man went.

'I'm afraid we're about to go in,' the Colonel told Jim. 'I really don't see how I might help you further.'

'I don't think you can, sir, thank you.'

'You'll keep us posted, won't you? Anything you can do to knock this whole sordid business on the head. Sorry – not the happiest choice of expression. You know what I mean?'

They shook hands and the Adjutant escorted Jim from the mess, back along the passageway whose walls were lined with regimental photographs. He paused before one and pointed. It was a head-and-shoulders photograph of a rugged-faced officer in active service tunic and a beret. The

165

eyes were piercing – the look of a man capable of outstaring danger.

'Colonel Kinthly, when he was a captain,' he said simply and indicated an adjoining frame. Under its glass was a citation for the award of the Military Cross to Captain J.C.G. Kinthly.

'Hardly the type, would you say?' the Adjutant suggested.

'I wouldn't have said so,' Jim agreed, then added casually, 'By the way, wasn't his son with the Regiment?'

'Peter? Still is. Captain.'

He noticed Jim's reaction and added, 'Couldn't introduce you. He's away on leave just now.'

They shook hands and Jim walked away and past the sentry at the main gate. The eyes in the photograph had settled it for him. When he had been left waiting in the lobby while the Adjutant was fetched he had looked idly at some other photographs on the walls. One of them had almost sprung out at him. It was captioned: 'Captain P. G. Kinthly, Individual Medal, Rifle Team, Bisley, 1978.' Another beside it showed the same young officer, this time captioned 'Revolver Team, 1979.' The face was that of the man who had seen Cropley off at Jersey Airport.

It was too late to try to get back to Heathrow in time for the last flight to Jersey. He booked into a modest hotel in Kensington, had a solitary dinner in an almost empty Italian restaurant round the corner, then turned in early.

As he thought about things over dinner he was in two minds whether he should have asked the Colonel or the Adjutant whether the name Cropley meant anything to them. From the man's soldierly appearance, and the obvious deference he had shown to Kinthly, Jim would bet odds he had served under him but was no longer in the army. On balance, though, he was glad he hadn't asked. While he couldn't conceive that Kinthly might have gone to the Island to frighten Furneaux off with any official or even off-the-record blessing, the less they knew of what Jim was by now suspecting, the less they might mention casually to him if he happened to arrive back soon. Jim had had to stop himself asking the Adjutant when that would be. In any case when Kinthly did get back they were certain to tell him that a Jersey policeman had been over asking questions. It would alert him enough.

Jim thought of going to call on Cropley there and then, but decided it could wait until morning. It made him impatient for the hours to pass, though, and he had a poor night, waking very early. By eight o'clock he had finished breakfast and was on the way by tube to Barons Court.

The paint shop was still locked. He went to the house door and rang the bell. After some moments Cropley answered it, chewing on his breakfast.

Jim said who he was and showed his I/D card. Cropley beckoned him in.

'Blimey, you lot get down to it early, don't you?' he said. 'You come over on this morning's flight?'

'No,' Jim replied, turning to look at him. 'Last night, for a mess evening at regimental HQ.'

He knew from the way the man's jaws stopped working abruptly that he had scored.

They were in a small kitchen with breakfast things scattered on the table. Cropley evidently lived alone.

'You an old soldier, or something?' he asked, recovering with an effort.

'Afraid not. How long did you do, Mr Cropley?'

The man's eyes were alive with suspicion now.

'Captain Kinthly a good officer, was he?' Jim asked calmly. He got his reaction again.

'Kinthly?'

'Do anything for him, would you? Help him fake an accident to put the mockers on Major Furneaux? Tell me, did you do it for money, or just old times' sake?'

Cropley took a step towards him. He seemed twice as broad as Jim.

'What the hell's your business, copper? Wait a minute – I get it! The old pals' act. That drunken Major's put the word to some pal to get the pressure taken off him. Well, you're not getting round me. He ran me down and I'm going to have him.'

Jim stayed rock still, talking on. 'Just chanced to meet up with Captain Kinthly in the Island, did you? Having a nice holiday, were you, till you had to cut it short? Nice place, Jersey, isn't it? Been there long, had you? Where were you staying?' He changed his tone from mockery to steely hardness. 'Don't try fooling me, Cropley. We can check it all.'

'You're bananas!' Cropley said, but he made no move to attack Jim, who was ready for him but knew what he would be up against.

'No, Cropley,' he answered, 'it's you who's bananas, letting him get you to do his work for him. Did that include Morton?'

Cropley blinked and stared.

'Who the hell's Morton?'

'The chap you laid out on the rocks to nick his briefcase.'

'I dunno what you're on about.'

'Oh, come on.'

'I never heard of any Morton. I never did nobody on any rocks.'

'You'll need to prove it.'

'You're bloody setting me up, aren't you? I've heard of your sort of fuzz.'

'Listen, Cropley, and answer this very carefully and accurately, because I can check it out all the way. Where were you during the late afternoon of the third?'

'No. I'm not falling for that. You're planning to work something round it.'

'I'm not planning to work anything. I want a straight answer, and it had better be the truth – unless you want to risk a murder charge.'

The man's mouth and eyes opened together in a grotesque stare.

'Murder? Who's talking about murder?'

'I am. Well, could be manslaughter, but that's bad enough. Morton, Cropley. On the rocks. Hit over the head.

Died yesterday in hospital – and all just to put a frightener on an old lush who thinks he has a story to sell.'

Cropley was licking dry lips. All the menace had left him. 'The . . . third?'

'Late Tuesday afternoon. After five. The time Morton was attacked.'

'I was here.'

'Care to prove it.'

'Yes, I bloody can. I got witnesses. Straight-up customers. I was working in me shop, polishing a bloke's car after I'd finished a respray job. He came round to collect it and another bloke was with him.'

'Pals of yours who'll say what they're expected to, of course.'

'No! I run this business legit, receipts, VAT and every bloody thing. It was an insurance job. There was forms, signed and dated.'

'A date lasts twenty-four hours. It could have been the morning. You could have been in the Island by late afternoon.'

'Look, I told you. All right, there was another bloke brought his car in quarter of an hour after they took that one away. It's down there now. I never seen him before. Check on him, if you want to. Listen, though – what's this about somebody getting done?'

Jim pulled one of the chairs back from the table and sat down, motioning Cropley to sit opposite him. He obeyed almost eagerly.

'You're sure the name Stanley Morton means nothing to you?'

'Never heard it, I told you.'

'He was helping Major Furneaux write a book about the Korean War.'

'Oh, that. I know about the book. It's why . . . Captain Kinthly told me about it. Something about his old man. Bloody mad about it. He wanted this Furneaux scared off. Said he'd tried it himself once, but the old chap had said he was still going on. The Captain thought up getting him done for drunk driving and hit-and-run. Sure of a stretch for that in Jersey, he said. That'd stop him, only he didn't want to get involved himself, because the old chap would spill all the beans to your people once he found who it was, and you might get suspicious. He phoned me to drop everything and fly over.'

'Done him a favour or two in the past, had you?'

'He's a hard bastard, Captain Kinthly. Anyone crosses him and he's bloody ruthless. I did a bookie over for him, only he recognised me and I got nicked. Suspended sentence, but I had to leave the Service.'

'And Captain Kinthly made it up to you. Helped set you up in business in gratitude for past and any future favours.'

'Something like that. But, listen, as honest as I sit here, I didn't do any Morton. I was here all Tuesday. Kinthly phoned me that night. I went over next day on a plane from Heathrow Wednesday. Check all you like, Sar'nt.'

Jim heard the ring of truth in this military-style appeal to his rank.

'Right, I'll believe you for now. You'll be hearing from us later about other matters. Meanwhile, if you want to do yourself a spot of good, you'll tell me anything else I ought to know about Kinthly and his intentions.'

'Straight, I dunno anything. He paid me off and told me to keep me mouth shut. So help me God, I hope you get hold of him before he hears I've been talking to you.'

Jim looked across at him with a new sharpness.

'What makes you say that?'

'I told you, he's bloody ruthless. Half-bonkers, you ask me, 'specially about his old man. You take my tip, Sarn't, and make sure old Furneaux's kept inside till Kinthly's off your bloody Island. And tell him whatever he hopes to make out of his bleedin' book, it won't be worth what else he'll get for it.'

'What's that supposed to mean?'

'What's it sound like? Believe me, mate, Kinthly won't stop at frighteners.'

Jim got up, looking at his watch. He could catch the 11.05 flight if he moved. He suddenly knew he had better be on it.

170

Chapter Twenty-Two

The tube sat stationary in a tunnel while the Heathrow-bound passengers fumed and fretted. Jim felt his nerves stretch. He'd hoped to get there in good time to telephone the Bureau with a warning. The odds were that Major Furneaux would have been allowed home on the previous evening, to await the hearing. There weren't long legal delays in the Jersey courts and he wasn't the type to skip the Island.

He thought he wouldn't manage it as he ran, breathing heavily, up the escalators. He heard the final call for British Airways flight 5132 to Jersey and tore to the desk. At least the aircraft wasn't full. He was the last aboard before the door was shut and the steps trundled away.

'Your leg really is better,' one of the stewardesses smiled. He recognised the girl who had been on that other flight back to the Island. He grinned back, but he wasn't in the mood for chit-chat.

'Mind if I get off first?' he asked her, when she and her colleague came round to collect the empty cups. His seat was far back in the aircraft.

'What, again!'

'All go in my job.'

She winked. When they had landed and were taxiing to the terminal the announcement came over that disembarkation would be by the rear door. He was right beside it.

'Good girl!' he told her as she stood back from the opened door to let him past. 'Buy you dinner some time.'

'You're on.'

He hurried to the terminal building and grabbed the nearest phone. Charlotte confirmed what he had expected. Major Furneaux had been allowed to go home in his own vehicle. She gave him his telephone number to save him looking it up.

'I'm afraid you've just missed him, Sergeant,' said a worried-sounding Mrs Furneaux who answered. 'He's just gone out.'

'Where? The Yacht Club?'

'No. Mr Voss telephoned.'

'Mr Voss?'

'His publisher. Oh, Sergeant, I'm so worried. My husband had another call last night, after you'd let him come home. It was someone threatening him if he went on with his book.'

'He wouldn't listen?'

'He told them nothing would stop him. I hoped, what with Mr Morton dying and all the notes being lost, he'd give it up. I said we'd manage about the money somehow. It isn't worth it. It isn't worth it!' She had begun to cry.

'Mrs Furneaux, please listen. I must know where your husband's gone. What's this about Mr Voss?'

'He was calling from his hotel. He said he's got all the tapes and notes back and wanted my husband to go there straightaway to discuss things. I begged him to refuse, but he wouldn't listen.'

'Did he say what hotel?'

'Yes. I thought Mr Voss had gone back to England, but evidently . . .'

'The hotel, Mrs Furneaux – which one?'

She told him, and he hung up without a goodbye.

He ran to his car and offended several other drivers by the way he cut them out as he drove from the car park. He would have to step on it to make the distance to the coastal hotel the other side of St Helier. Even if Voss had come back to the Island so soon he would never have put up at a place so far removed from the chief concentrations of hotels. Major Furneaux must be confused – or perhaps half-sozzled again – to have believed it.

Jim drove by the main roads. There was more risk of being stopped and delayed by a patrol for speeding, but so long as he wasn't he could get on above the speed limit instead of having to risk a head-on smash on some minor way. He kept

172

his eyes peeled for the Land Rover he had seen in the Bureau compound.

Jim wished he had an R/T set. He wished to hell they would stop pussyfooting about and reinstate him properly, so that he could have squad cars on tap instead of having to use his unequipped Triumph. Still, she could go, and that was what mattered now.

He was within a mile of his destination when he saw an old Land Rover parked at the roadside. A small hire car was parked in front of it. He slowed and saw at once the Rover's damaged headlamp and wing. He reversed the Triumph in behind it and jumped out.

It was a part of the coast overlooking St Clement's Bay, beyond the golf course. There were no houses or other buildings here and no other cars parked. Rocks stretched seaward, left bare by the low tide to glisten in the sun like some pitted white moonscape, and just as deserted.

There was a small cliff overhang below where he was standing. He went cautiously to the edge of it and braced himself to lean over. He got a glimpse of a head of short-cut fair hair and jerked himself back, to get down on his stomach and listen.

The slight surf was far off and he could hear clearly the Major's angry voice.

'I didn't think the Regiment would sink to this, Kinthly. Or is it your own mad idea? Your father's blood coming out?'

'Don't speak of my father,' a younger voice commanded. 'Do you know what he used to call you? "Furnothing". That's what he and the rest thought of you. Incompetent, jealous, twisted, despicable.'

'At least I never murdered innocent civilians. Mowed them down in cold blood . . .'

'You know that's just your twisted bloody lie. Concocted out of your sick mind to make money. Well, I'm glad I got to hear of it in time. You'll never make your filth public now.'

'You harm me, Kinthly, and you'll draw even more attention to the story – which, by the way, is true. I saw it. I was there.'

'Lying bastard! I tell you there'll be no story, Furneaux, because your notes are all destroyed and you won't be alive to start again. No prospects, no money, court case coming up, certain jail sentence, disgrace... They'll say, "no wonder the old soak found a lonely place and blew his brains out." '

It was enough for Jim. He launched himself over the lip of the cliff in a nose-dive which brought him crashing between them. As he recovered himself he saw Major Furneaux move quickly and violently to knock out of the younger man's hand the revolver he was holding. Kinthly retaliated with a blow that sent the Major sprawling. He reached down for his gun, but Jim's foot was on it.

'Stand still, Captain Kinthly,' he ordered. 'You're under arrest.'

From the wild look in the man's eyes – a glitter he easily recognised from the portrait of his father – he thought he was going to be jumped. He fished out his I/D card and held it up like a talisman.

Kinthly continued to glare back; but suddenly he let his hands drop to his sides. A gleam of tears appeared, to quench the anger in his eyes.

'It isn't true,' he said, shaking his head. 'Not my father. Never.'

Jim's eye caught the Major's. He returned a grimace and a shrug expressive of helplessness, but said nothing.

Jim picked up the revolver, applied the safety catch, and stuffed it in his pocket.

'Come on, Captain,' he said and took Kinthly's arm, to direct him to the nearest cliff path. The Major followed, silent, shaken and dejected.

'Hello, stranger,' Francine greeted him when he went home to the vineyard that evening. She came into his arms for a long kiss.

'I haven't started a meal because I didn't know whether

you would be coming,' she said at length. 'I was going to make do with a bowl of soup and some cheese.'

'How about lobster instead?' he suggested.

'Lobster! Any time. Where?'

'The Barge. Where else? Lil's started taking a proprietary interest in us two, do you know?'

Lil had indeed. Her brassy exterior hid a deeply romantic nature. The happiness in the faces of the handsome man and the beautiful girl as they took bar stools to await their meal brought joy to her warm heart. All the same, she affected to complain.

'Dammit, Jim, it's not like old times. How can I offer you an orange squash on the house?'

'Try me. I might even accept.'

Francine made up for it by accepting an enormous Pernod.

'Well?' she asked, as they raised their glasses to one another. 'What are we celebrating? Have you passed your medical board?'

He shook his head. 'Still not fixed.'

'Then, is this some special occasion?'

'They're all becoming special with you, Frankie.' Then he added seriously, 'I've been to London since I saw you last. Being in a plane again brought a lot back – Tom and everything. Landing here this morning was a bit like going back to Square One. Only this time I felt it was you I was coming home to.'

She looked searchingly into his eyes.

'Jim – I have been wondering what is for the best. To stay or to go?'

'You can guess my answer to that.'

'You have made it so much easier for me. I couldn't have borne to stay here, but for you.'

'I'd like to think it's because of me you'll decide to.'

She took his hand, unknowingly echoing Voss's exact words when Jim had insisted on their meal here being a Dutch Treat.

'See how we get on, shall we?'

The parallel didn't escape him.

'*Et voilà!*' announced Gulliver in his West Country French, proudly bringing out their starters, a magnificent display of *Fruits de Mer* on a silver dish.

They went to their table hand in hand.